***'Twas***
*the ...*

Unlike the rhy... rarely have the luxury of quiet moments, but whichever ward or clinic is involved they all share in the anticipation and excitement building up to the joys of Christmas Day.

Our four books this month are set in hospitals during Christmas Eve, when emotions are heightened, and our heroes and heroines are, unexpectedly or not, forced to confront their real feelings. We visit Casualty, Maternity, Intensive Care and Paediatrics, and in the dark hours of the night touch on sadness, humour and joy, before facing the dawn of a wonderful new day.

***Merry Christmas!***

**Josie Metcalfe** lives in Cornwall now with her long-suffering husband, four children and two horses, but, as an army brat frequently on the move, books became the only friends who came with her wherever she went. Now that she writes them herself she is making new friends, and hates saying goodbye at the end of a book—but there are always more characters in her head clamouring for attention until she can't wait to tell their stories.

**Recent titles by the same author:**

# INSTANT FATHER CHRISTMAS

BY
## JOSIE METCALFE

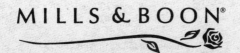
MILLS & BOON®

MILLS & BOON and MILLS & BOON with the Rose Device
are registered trademarks of the publisher.

First published in Great Britain 1998
Harlequin Mills & Boon Limited,
Eton House, 18-24 Paradise Road, Richmond, Surrey TW9 1SR

© Josie Metcalfe 1998

ISBN 0 263 81255 3

Set in Times Roman 10½ on 12 pt.
03-9812-49767-D

Printed and bound in Norway
by AIT Trondheim AS, Trondheim

# CHAPTER ONE

'IT CAN'T *still* be snowing!' Livvy groaned over the drifting sound of Christmas carols when she glanced out of the window on her way back to the ward.

'Don't you believe it,' croaked Aled Parry, his voice almost non-existent as he fought the bug going the rounds in the hospital. 'I don't know who put in the special request with the Almighty for a white Christmas, but he's certainly delivering a lot of it! It looks as we're going to be properly snowed in—and on Christmas Eve, too.'

Livvy scolded, 'In fact, you shouldn't be here at all. You've come back to work far too soon, if you feel as bad as you look.'

'Whereas you, Livvy Jones, look as if you're absolutely blooming,' he said with heavy-handed gallantry, the musical drift of his Welsh accent only just discernible through his sore throat.

'If you mean blooming enormous, I'd agree.' She smoothed one hand over the prominent bulge of her pregnancy with a grimace as they made their way along the corridor. 'I look like a beached whale.'

'If the other whales look as sexy as you, I don't know why there hasn't been a whale population explosion.'

'The only explosion around here will be mine if I don't get to a bathroom soon,' she grumbled. 'Now that the head has engaged it feels as if my bladder has been squashed to the capacity of a thimble.'

'Well, I'm just hoping you don't decide to go into labour any time in the next week,' the young registrar retorted in his painfully scratchy voice. 'The whole hospital's in absolute chaos with the flu epidemic. It was bad enough with it being Christmas week, but then this freaky snow coming so early…'

'That's why Duncan French made the decision to call in the mums who were very close to delivery,' Livvy pointed out with a wry thumb at herself. 'Although it isn't far as the crow flies, some of us live in very isolated areas. If we were cut off from the rest of the world by snow and then went into labour we could end up with a disaster.'

'Well, I want it to go on record that I don't approve of you working,' Aled said firmly. 'You stopped work over a month ago and you're supposed to be on maternity leave, waiting for your own delivery, not helping us out here.'

'I *am* on leave. I wouldn't be here if it weren't for the danger of being isolated,' Livvy reminded him, swatting at a bunch of festive balloons as she passed. 'Anyway, apart from looking as if I've swallowed a very large watermelon, I'm feeling fine. I certainly couldn't sit around, twiddling my thumbs, while the department's so busy and short of staff.'

'As long as you leave all the heavy work to the rest of us and keep your feet up as much as possible,' he warned with a shake of a stern finger as he paused beside her outside the toilets. 'Say your prayers that the next two days are utterly peaceful and remember… I'll be keeping an eye on you.'

Livvy heard his raw cough, receding along the corridor as the door swung closed behind him, and winced.

'If you're still on *your* feet,' she muttered as she made a dive for the nearest cubicle. She knew he should really have taken several more days off work before he returned, but the staffing levels were becoming desperate, especially as the epidemic was causing more and more of the vulnerable surrounding population to be admitted for care.

Not that she minded spending her time on the wards— far from it. It was lovely to be surrounded by the hustle and bustle of the wards after the enforced peace and quiet of the last few weeks since she'd stopped work.

She'd been employed on this combined unit for over six months before she went on maternity leave, dividing her time between the maternity section on one floor and the obs and gynae on the next, and it had come to feel more like home than her own home did.

Livvy thought of the tiny cottage she'd left late yesterday afternoon, picturing the tiny artificial tree sitting forlornly beside the fireplace and the meagre pile of presents underneath it—mostly gifts for the baby from her colleagues.

Knowing that a couple of them had half promised to visit over the holiday period, she'd bought a packet of baubles and tinsel, but it had hardly seemed worth the effort of doing any more decorating than that when she would probably be the only one to see it.

The unhappy shadow of loneliness started to encroach and she deliberately pushed it away.

Livvy certainly hadn't intended to become a single mum, but as that had seemed to be the only choice open to her for her baby's sake she would make a darned good job of it. Next year she would have her baby's first

Christmas to celebrate, and with two of them everything would be different.

She couldn't prevent a quick mental image of Daniel's face, flashing across her mind's eye, a wicked twinkle in his eye as he stole a kiss under the mistletoe last year, and her heart clenched.

Most of the time she could force herself to stop thinking about him, but she knew that was mainly because, since she'd moved to Bryn Madoc Memorial, she never saw him any more. If this baby she carried was born with her own blue-grey eyes and blonde hair everything would be all right. If it had inherited Daniel's blue-eyed, dark good looks it would be so much harder to forget the person from whom they'd been inherited.

She tugged her outsized uniform smock over the bulge and when she smoothed her hand over it was rewarded by a hefty kick.

'Hey, you!' she murmured softly as she ran her finger over the outline of something pointed and bony. 'All the books say you should be moving around a lot less by this stage, but I suppose they forgot to tell you that!'

She was still smiling at the energetic contortions going on inside her as she returned to the maternity ward to check up on her charges.

'Anybody had their baby while I was gone?' she asked when she joined the group congregated in the chairs surrounding the television set at one end of the ward, and received a chorus of groans in reply.

'It's obvious you didn't either!' quipped Megan Williams, one of the older women waiting more or less patiently for something to happen. Two of the group had come in yesterday afternoon, apparently in the first stages of labour, but nothing much had happened since they'd arrived.

In more normal circumstances they would be on their way back home by now to wait for further developments, but the weather being what it was...

'Where have all the men gone?' Livvy asked when she realised belatedly that it was just the women left on the ward.

'They decided they wanted to watch the TV action adventure film, starting in a few minutes, so they've gone to find another set in the visitors' waiting room,' Megan explained.

'So, what are you watching here?' Livvy angled herself so that she could focus on the screen, surrounded by a forest of Christmas cards, and saw characters in Regency period dress.

'My Christmas present,' said Alwyn Morgan, the youngest of the group, around whom the rest of them had gathered.

She was the only one actually lying on her bed because of the monitor leads, snaking away from the belt around her to the blinking box of technology on a trolley beside the bed.

Livvy stifled the grin that tried to surface when she saw the big tinsel bow decorating the top of the high-tech pale grey box. That was probably Megan's doing, she thought as she glanced around at the glittery additions that had appeared all around the room since the bubbly woman had arrived this morning. Tinsel and baubles seemed to be dangling from anything that had stood still long enough.

'It's the film of Jane Austen's *Pride and Prejudice*,' she explained with a cheerful grin. 'My husband, Phil, brought the machine from home when he brought my things in, but the men didn't want to watch it with us— probably couldn't stand seeing us drooling over Mr Darcy.'

Livvy joined in the laughter. 'I wasn't certain he was the right actor for the part when I first saw it,' she commented, remembering how she'd always imagined the character as somehow leaner and more aristocratic-looking...more like Daniel...

She dragged her thoughts away from forbidden territory.

'I thought the same, but he grew on me,' said Megan, and for a moment Livvy thought she was talking about Daniel.

'He certainly looks like the sort of man a woman could depend on,' Nerys Owens added with a dreamy expression on her freckled twenty-something face, her eyes riveted to the screen. 'He seems like the sort of man who doesn't fall in love easily, but when he does you know it'll be for ever.'

Livvy joined in the renewed laughter but hers had a hollow ring. She'd once thought the same about Daniel, but had learned the hard way how wrong she could be.

'Well, if you're all quite happy drooling over Mr Darcy, I'll take myself off for a quick trip round the rest of the department. There'll be someone in Sister's office if anyone needs anything before I get back.'

'You're still hoping you get to do another delivery before you have to go through it yourself,' Megan taunted with the experience of a couple of previous deliveries of her own behind her. 'All book-learning, you. About time you took your practical exam!'

There was genuine laughter on her face when Livvy

left the maternity ward to go and check up on the other patients, and her heartache at the memory of Daniel's betrayal had eased a little as it was pushed to the back of her mind by the work in hand.

She waited under a bunch of balloons for the lift to take her to the next floor, silently groaning when she remembered how easily she had once run up and down the stairs. Sometimes it felt as if she was never going to be able to see her feet again...

By coincidence, she'd been at the hospital yesterday for what she had hoped was her last antenatal check-up before her baby was born. The weather had already been turning bad when she'd driven in and when the met. office had predicted worse her obstetrician had decided it would be safer for her and her baby if she abandoned her isolated little cottage and stayed at the hospital.

She'd argued that her due date was still ten days off but Duncan French had been adamant.

'You can always occupy yourself by criticising your erstwhile colleagues,' he'd suggested, and Livvy had brightened.

'If you're going to call in all the mums most likely to deliver you're going to need extra hands,' she'd commented with subtle guile, knowing that her wistfulness would be obvious.

For a moment it had looked as if he'd been going to object to the mere idea of her helping out in her advanced stage of pregnancy, but at the last minute he'd laughed.

'You wouldn't be able to sit still if I chained you to the bed, would you?' he said in resigned tones. 'Well, as long as you're only an extra, unofficial member of staff and don't have sole responsibility for any ward in particular...'

'I could act as a sort of liaison between the two wards, helping out where necessary,' she volunteered eagerly, her crossed fingers hidden in the voluminous folds of her maternity smock.

He sighed heavily.

'At least there'll be people around to keep an eye on you, in spite of the flu cutting a swathe through the staff,' he grumbled.

At this time of year Livvy knew that it was hospital policy to try to send home everyone who was fit to go so that they could spend Christmas with their families. Theoretically, this also had the effect of allowing as many staff as possible to have some time off.

Unfortunately, this year everything had descended into chaos with the empty beds in both the maternity and obs and gynae wards now filled with the full-term patients they'd called in as a precautionary measure.

It wouldn't have been so bad if the snow still falling steadily outside had waited to arrive until the worst of the flu epidemic had passed, but on Christmas Eve? Now they faced full wards in almost every department and barely enough staff, and there was little prospect of either situation changing.

Still, the work Livvy was doing, although necessary in the circumstances, had been uneventful.

So far this had meant making a circuit of each area for a supervisory chat with the nurses, and a more social visit with each of the patients while she updated their charts.

At first she had worried that the staff might have resented her presence, but so far they'd all been delighted to welcome her back.

'Hi, Livvy. No problems here—apart from lack of bed space. Any minute now we're going to have to start making a waiting list,' called Staff Nurse Sue Tarrant when she caught sight of Livvy making her ponderous way along the corridor.

'Waiting list?' Livvy questioned. 'Since when? I thought we were keeping pace with things.'

'We've had a call to say that a young woman, visiting relatives in the area for Christmas, has gone into labour three weeks early. She should be here within the hour to take up the last available bed.'

'Will we have any of her antenatal records?' Livvy worried aloud, focusing on the problems she could do something about rather than the ones she couldn't.

'The hospital is contacting the place she was booked to attend and they'll be doing a computer transfer.'

'Well, keep your fingers crossed that both arrive in time and in the right order,' Livvy said fervently. 'I don't really want to be in the position of delivering someone without any idea of their past history.'

'I'll keep you posted,' Sue promised. 'Shall I let you know as soon as she arrives?'

'Please.' Livvy frowned slightly, mentally sorting through the things she would have to do before the woman arrived. 'In the meantime, I'll make certain the computer knows we haven't got any more space up here and check that the delivery suite is ready.'

'I know she's only three weeks premature but do you think we ought to make certain there's a crib ready in the special care baby unit?' Sue suggested.

'That was going to be my next port of call,' Livvy

confirmed wryly. 'So far we've only got word of mouth telling us she's three weeks early. I'd rather be prepared for every eventuality than have to do everything in a panic if we find she's really three *months* prem.'

'Don't even think it!' exclaimed Sue. 'That's the stuff of nightmares, especially with the numbers we've got in the hospital at the moment. How are they doing downstairs?'

'Nothing was moving when I left there a few minutes ago, apart from a bit of heavy breathing as they settled down to watch Mr Darcy in *Pride and Prejudice*.'

'Mmm! I know what you mean. What that man does for a wet shirt ought to be illegal!' Sue said with a laugh and a wiggle of her eyebrows. 'Unfortunately, all quiet a few minutes ago doesn't mean anything with full-term mums.'

'Especially when they hear about the one coming in,' Livvy pointed out. 'Sometimes the fact that one of them is in labour seems to trigger others off!'

'As long as it doesn't have the same effect on you, or we *will* be stuck! You know that Amy's been feeling a bit rough since she came on duty today?'

Livvy's heart sank with dread.

Amy Aldarini was the most senior and most experienced midwife on duty, and if she went sick at the same time as several of their patients went into strong labour at once...

Livvy drew in a deep breath and rubbed her hands over her face.

'I refuse to think about it,' she said firmly. 'It's just sheer bad luck that the flu jabs we had don't seem to be fully effective against the strain that's hit us. Usually, enough of us can keep going to run things more or less smoothly but, coming on top of the snow...'

'Forget about that for now,' Sue advised. 'I'll give her a gallon or two of orange juice to bump up her vitamins while you check that everything's ready for the lady on her way in.'

'That's always supposing she gets here if the roads are as bad as the reports suggest,' Livvy said. 'She could end up having it in a police car if they get stuck somewhere.'

'Wouldn't be the first one,' Sue said with a farewell wave, resignation in her voice.

Livvy stepped out of the lift and saw the member of staff in question, walking towards her around the corner.

'Amy, Sue told me you weren't feeling too well. How are you now?' she asked, noting the other woman's pale face with trepidation. Her pallor hardly went with the red tinsel bow pinned to the front of her uniform.

'Awful, if you want the truth,' her colleague admitted honestly. 'The only good thing about it is that I'm not going down with flu so I won't be infecting anyone and you won't be losing me halfway through my shift.'

'Are you sure? Everyone's been dropping like flies.'

'I can be absolutely certain because I've just had the result of a pregnancy test,' she said a little smugly after a quick look around to see who might be listening.

'Congratulations!' Livvy said with an answering grin and a quick squeeze of her slender arm. 'I know you and Antonio were hoping to start a family fairly soon.'

'At our age we haven't got as much time to waste as other newly-weds,' she said candidly. 'In fact, once I passed thirty-four I had finally resigned myself to remaining single. Now, within the space of three months,

I've met the man of my dreams, married him and we're already starting a family!'

Happiness absolutely radiated out of her willowy frame and Livvy had to squash down a quick surge of envy. Once she'd thought that she had everything, too, and within just a few short weeks everything had fallen apart...

'As long as you're certain that everything's OK?' Livvy prompted when she'd dragged her thoughts ruthlessly back to the present.

'As OK as they can be when I turn green at the slightest thing,' Amy complained. 'I was hardly a week pregnant when I started feeling queasy, and if it lasts right up until the usual three months I'll have faded to a shadow.'

'Don't make me jealous,' Livvy joked as she glanced pointedly down at her non-existent waistline. 'But seriously, make certain you take the time to raid the biscuits. The tin is usually half full of the plain ones that everyone else leaves till last, and it's amazing how much nibbling on them can help.'

'I've been too worried about being sick to try it, but if you recommend it I'll give it a go. I've been telling expectant mums to do it for years but I didn't know whether it was one of those old wives' tales. Anyway, I was feeling too green to dare.'

'It's one of the ones that seems to work, at least it did for me. In the meantime, have you heard about the prem. mum on her way in?'

'When? Whose is she—one of mine?' Amy asked, referring to the new system Bryn Madoc Memorial had begun of assigning each pregnant woman to a particular midwife.

'No. She's a complete stranger on a visit to her husband's relatives in the area for Christmas. We're waiting for her antenatal notes to be transferred from her own hospital.'

'Let's hope they arrive in time to do some good, then,' Amy said with her fingers firmly crossed. 'The delivery suite's all ready to go. Do you want me to check up on the special care baby unit, just in case? It was cleaned from top to bottom first thing this morning after little Stephen Fisher was transferred to the special cardiac unit in Cardiff, but I could just cast an eye over it to make certain we're ready for every eventuality.'

'Please. That would be great,' Livvy said with a grateful smile. 'Everything's in such a muddle, with both the obs and gynae *and* maternity wards full of pregnant mums. With any luck, the snow will be short-lived and the highways authorities will be able to clear the roads so everyone can go home in a day or so. I'll be happier when everything's back in order again.'

'I'm just glad we were able to send the last lot of mothers and babies to spend Christmas at home or there'd really be standing room only. Let's hope the last thirty-six hours without a delivery isn't the lull before the storm,' Amy said, crossing her fingers again. 'It will probably be a very jolly Christmassy atmosphere today and tomorrow with the number we've packed in, but if they all decided to go into labour at the same time...'

'Bite your tongue!' Livvy exclaimed. 'Don't even think it!' She gave a theatrical shudder then looked at her watch. 'I'm going to have to dash to the toilet again before I make my way back down to Pat. In spite of what I said, I've got a funny feeling about a couple of the mums down there.'

'Just tell them to keep their legs crossed!' Amy joked frivolously.

'That won't work for them any more than it would for me,' Livvy pointed out as she set off rapidly towards the ladies' toilets, cursing that second cup of tea.

She smiled wryly. Over the last few months she had come to know, almost to the last pace, exactly how far she was from the nearest toilet at any given moment. She'd known dogs to take less notice of trees than she did of the hospital's public conveniences...

'Sister!' called Megan Williams, surreptitiously beckoning her over almost as soon as Livvy appeared in the doorway of the maternity ward.

'Problems?' Livvy asked quietly, picking up an air of tension about the usually upbeat woman. 'Are you feeling all right?'

'It's not me, it's Nerys,' the older woman murmured under the cover of the video, still playing on the television. 'She hasn't said anything but I've noticed that she's glancing at the clock about every ten minutes and her breathing alters. She's due for another one in the next couple of minutes if I'm right.'

Livvy surreptitiously watched the younger woman under the guise of watching the film and saw what Megan meant.

'Well spotted. Have you ever thought of becoming a detective?' she joked. 'She probably doesn't want to say anything until she's certain it isn't another false alarm,' she continued calmly. 'Shall I leave you to keep an eye on her for me? I don't want to put any stress on her if she's coping all right.'

'There's plenty of time before the rest of the group needs to know what's happening,' Megan agreed, apparently delighted to be asked to help but concerned about her young charge. 'Poor kid. I can remember how scared I was with *my* first. My aunties had fed me on a solid nine-month diet of childbirth horror-stories before I got to that stage.'

'At least she's got someone like you to give her confidence,' Livvy said, watching the freckled face grow paler as Nerys closed her eyes and concentrated on her breathing. She carefully looked away before the young woman's eyes opened again. 'Just call me if you notice anything you think I should know.'

'You'll be doing your round of the charts in the near future, anyway,' Megan said. 'I'll tip you the wink if she looks like she needs you and she's too shy to say anything before then.'

Livvy gave her shoulder a silent squeeze and left the group to their appreciation of Mr Darcy's aristocratic charms.

She made her way towards Sister's office, suddenly conscious that all the charging around she'd been doing seemed to have given her an ache low down in her back. What she needed was a few minutes with her feet up and with the hospital central heating roaring away to combat the bitter cold outside, she was desperately in need of another cup of tea. She was too thirsty at the moment to care about the resulting trips to the bathroom.

'Is the kettle on?' she asked as she joined Pat Lersh out of hearing of the musical accompaniment to the video being played at the other end of the ward.

'Are you gasping?' Pat said with a grin as she reached across to flick the switch. 'The air in here is very dry when the heating's turned up so high.'

Livvy glanced up at the clock, having to peer at it

through the dangling strands of tinsel. 'Is that really the time? Where has the morning gone? Don't tell our nice young Dr Parry, but it's been several hours since I last put my feet up.'

'Aled? Is he here?' Pat said in a studiously nonchalant voice totally at odds with the quick blush staining her pale skin.

'Not yet,' Livvy said, stifling a grin of amusement at the staff nurse's poorly hidden attraction. The two of them had been warily circling each other for a couple of months, now, with neither of them apparently willing to make the first move. 'But you can bet he'll appear as soon as I do something he disapproves of. He's just waiting for a chance to make me take things easy.'

She squirmed awkwardly in her seat to settle the lumpy cushion in just the right place in the small of her back, hoping it would relieve the niggling ache she'd developed.

'You must admit, it isn't very often that the nursing staff are more pregnant than the patients,' Pat pointed out with a laugh as she handed Livvy a steaming mug and held the open biscuit tin towards her.

Livvy sipped appreciatively, before cradling the mug gingerly on top of her bulge and slipping her shoes off to wriggle her toes.

'Oh, that's good,' she sighed as she tipped her head back. 'Just to sit back and relax peacefully with a cup of tea I haven't had to make for myself.'

She'd barely finished speaking when the phone rang and she groaned when her young colleague silently deferred to her to take the call.

'You answer it, Pat. You're officially on duty.

Besides, I don't want to heave myself out of the chair yet.'

'Maternity. Staff Nurse Lersh,' Pat responded smartly, the smile on her face evident in the tone of her voice.

As Livvy watched it was replaced by a frown of concern.

'She's arrived? Yes. We've been expecting her to— Oh. Another one? But we haven't got any more—' The person on the other end was obviously interrupting her every time she spoke. 'Have you checked with Obs and Gynae? I thought they had a couple of spare places.'

Without needing to ask, Livvy knew that someone was in search of a bed and, having recently spoken to Amy, knew what the answer would be.

The full capacity of each ward under her overall supervision was actually greater than the number of patients currently in them, but there were only so many qualified staff fit to take care of the necessary nursing duties. If they were forced to take in more than the safe limit it could be a recipe for disaster, especially if any more of them went into labour during the next few hours. They already had one lady on her way in, and now Nerys was having contractions.

Pat finished the call and put the phone down with a grimace, but before she could tell Livvy the bad news there was the sound of rapid footsteps, crossing the ward towards them. There was a tap on the door and it was hesitantly pushed open halfway.

'Is Sister there?' puffed Caroline Woolford, one of the ladies who had come in as a false alarm earlier that morning.

She caught sight of Livvy. 'I'm sorry to disturb you, Sister, but Megan said her waters just broke.'

'Tell her I'm on my way,' Livvy said, and threw an exasperated smile towards the nervous first-timer as she started to struggle out of the squashy upholstery. 'At least, I will be if this chair ever lets me escape!'

'I think we spoke too soon,' Pat said as she offered both hands to pull Livvy to her feet. 'Everything's suddenly getting far too lively. That call was to tell us that there are two patients on their way up to us.'

'Two?' Livvy was dismayed but her mind quickly started computing the extra arrangements they would have to make, from checking linens to ordering extra food.

'One of them we were already expecting—the lady visiting family in the area. She's going upstairs. There aren't any hospital notes yet but, apparently, she *is* only three weeks early and hasn't progressed very far so we might be lucky.'

'And the other one?' Livvy prompted.

'She's down in Casualty. Part of a wedding party involved in a road accident. She's about two and a half months pregnant and worried about a miscarriage. Aled's just seen her and told them to send her up. He wants her to have a scan and be kept under observation for a while.'

'Poor woman,' Livvy murmured as one hand smoothed protectively over her own baby. Her situation might not be ideal but she would be devastated if anything were to happen to deprive her of her child.

'Would you like to ring them upstairs to see if they can take both of them?' Pat suggested. 'If Nerys and Megan are both in labour we're going to be pushed if we've got a miscarriage on our hands as well. That's without the mental trauma to the patient when she's threatened with losing her own baby while surrounded by full-term mums.'

'I think you're right. It'll be harder for us to cope with a third mother—the holiday visitor—in labour, but at least upstairs none of them are already in labour.'

Livvy reached for the phone but it rang under her hand.

'Maternity. Sister Jones,' she said automatically. Pat waved to catch her attention and pointed to the ward to let her know where she was going. Livvy nodded and turned to concentrate on her call as Pat left the room.

'Hello, Livvy. Sue Tarrant here on Obs and Gynae,' said the voice on the other end. 'Any chance you could take a couple of bodies down there or can you spare one of your nurses for a couple of hours? Our holiday visitor has just arrived up here and her contractions have just speeded up to four minutes and it looks like two more of our ladies are in labour.'

'Oh, glory be! Sorry, Sue. I was just about to phone to ask you the same thing. I've just had a threatened miscarriage arrive, one of mine is having regular contractions and another has just had her waters burst. It looks as though we're both going to have to muddle through. I'll check to see if we can borrow some willing hands from elsewhere but I think it's pretty much the same situation right through the hospital.'

Sue groaned.

'All we can do now is keep our fingers crossed that they all have relatively short straightforward labours and we'll be all right. Have you been in touch with Duncan?'

'That's the next job on my list,' Livvy said, hoping the consultant was still in the hospital. He lived fairly close by and had been known to dive off home for a couple of hours to eat a home-cooked meal or catch up on sleep. She dialled and crossed the fingers of her free hand that he'd decided to brave a hospital meal this time. It looked as if they were going to need him today.

No one seemed to know where Duncan French had gone so Livvy was forced to try to impress on the frazzled voice on the other end of the phone the urgency of getting in contact with him.

She'd just got hold of Sue and passed on the news when she heard the ward doors lock back to announce the arrival of the new patient. 'Got to go, Sue. The patient's arrived and I need to get her settled down and calm as soon as possible. Keep me posted.'

Livvy tugged the hem of her smock down over her bulge as she walked across the room towards the door, her eyes quickly scanning the figure in the wheelchair.

What she could see of her was swathed in one of Casualty's blankets, the folds clutched around her by a slender hand, wearing a stunning set of rings.

The rest of her was half-hidden behind the man who was bending over her solicitously, his short, dark hair a stark contrast to her slightly bedraggled honey-gold curls.

'Hello, I'm Sister Jones,' she said, and the man straightened to his full height beside the wheelchair and turned to face her as the two of them looked in her direction. 'I'm sorry, but we don't yet know your... name...'

Her voice trailed away in disbelief, the words trapped in her throat as she recognized the man who had been pushing the chair.

Pain clenched around her heart like a tight fist as, for the first time in nearly seven months, she met her husband's clear blue eyes.

# CHAPTER TWO

'DANIEL,' she mouthed silently, her eyes widening in disbelief as she helplessly catalogued the lean elegance of his dark good looks.

If she wasn't mistaken, he was wearing the same classic dark suit he'd worn to their wedding, the fit across his unexpectedly broad shoulders just as perfect as ever.

But it was his deep blue eyes that drew her attention back, and when their gazes meshed again she completely forgot how to breathe as her heart leapt into her throat.

He had always had that effect on her, from the very first time they'd met on her first day on the maternity ward at St Augustine's…but there was no time to think about that now, not when his unsmiling face was filled with a mixture of indecipherable expressions.

'Livvy?' he questioned hoarsely, his eyes going from her face to the blatant evidence of her advanced pregnancy and back again in open disbelief.

For just a moment she found herself regretting the fact that she hadn't informed him she was expecting their child but then his companion spoke and the regret was wiped out by a familiar bitterness.

'Daniel? Shouldn't I be having this test?' prompted the woman seated in the wheelchair between them, her hand still visibly trembling from the aftermath of the accident as it came up to grasp Daniel's. 'How quickly will they be able to tell if the baby's all right?'

When she saw the familiar way the other woman drew

Daniel's attention Livvy suddenly realised where she'd seen her before.

'Alice Webster,' she murmured as the events of that dreadful day seven months ago assailed her. *This* was the woman who'd been responsible for the destruction of her marriage. *This* was the woman who had stolen Daniel away…who had given birth to his…

'Jones now,' she corrected Livvy, looking up at Daniel with a smile full of happiness in spite of her bedraggled state. 'It's Alice *Jones* as of ten o'clock this morning.' She held up her other hand to display the gleaming ring on her finger.

The emotional blow was so fierce that Livvy swayed and had to take one staggering step back before she realised that she'd done it. It was Daniel's quickly outstretched hand that jerked her back into control before he could touch her.

'Well, Mrs Jones, if you'd like to come this way.'

Livvy managed to choke the words out, but wasn't capable of saying any more so she turned on her heel as quickly as her bulk would allow and led the way towards the other side of the ward and the waiting bed.

She was able to distract herself for a moment by busily checking that the bed was ready and drawing the curtains around to provide a little privacy.

Unfortunately, that didn't take nearly long enough for her to regain her equilibrium but far too long when she measured the endless aeons she seemed to be spending in close proximity with Daniel and his new wife.

It was raw torture to watch the caring way he helped the shaken woman out of the wheelchair and onto the bed. She could remember only too clearly what it had felt like to be cradled in the powerful warmth of his arms and had revelled in the way he'd seemed to delight in taking care of her.

When she heard him asking the *new* Mrs Jones if she needed any help to take her clothes off Livvy knew she couldn't stand watching them together any more, especially when he made a light-hearted joke about their clothing being full of confetti and rice.

'I'll leave you to get settled while I fetch a file for Mrs Jones,' she said, all too aware that her voice sounded strained. Before either of them could comment on her abrupt departure she had whisked the curtain closed behind her and was hurrying as fast as she could manage towards the office.

'How *could* he?' she muttered fiercely under her breath as she paced awkwardly between the desk and the filing cabinet. 'How could he have come *here*?'

The words seemed to linger in the close confines of the room and she was tempted to giggle hysterically when she heard how ridiculous they sounded.

As if Daniel had *chosen* to have an accident on his wedding day just to upset her! As if he had thought about her at all in the last seven months! He certainly hadn't bothered to let her know that the divorce had been finalised, leaving him free to marry the mother of his son. And now, if all went well in spite of the accident, there was to be another child...

She wrapped her arms as far as they would reach around her own precious baby. The painful sob trapped in her chest was fighting to escape but she couldn't afford to let it happen—if she started crying now she probably wouldn't stop for days.

She managed to fight off the press of tears but she

couldn't stop the memories crowding in on her...the precious memories of the first time she'd met Daniel.

She had been part way through her nursing training at St Augustine's and it had been her first day on Maternity, with Mr den Haag due to arrive on his rounds at any moment.

There had been some sort of mix-up in a message to Housekeeping and they had run short of bed linen. As the newest member of staff, Sister had sent her at the run to collect an armful of freshly laundered sheets. It wouldn't have done for the ward to be untidy when the consultant arrived.

Not that Mr den Haag had been any sort of an ogre—quite the contrary. Sister had been at great pains to tell her that he was such a genuinely caring man that everyone automatically wanted to do their best for him.

The lift had been full of patients on trolleys so she'd been forced to gallop the long way up the stairs. She had just been hurrying round a corner in the corridor with her arms full of freshly laundered sheets when she'd ploughed straight into an immovable object.

'Careful!' The slightly husky tenor voice carried the lilt of laughter as his lean hands steadied her.

She looked up into eyes the same clear blue as an early morning summer sky and was lost.

'I...I'm sorry,' she stammered, feeling the heat of embarrassment spread up her throat and into her cheeks.

'I'm not,' he murmured softly, making no effort to release her even though she was no longer in any danger of falling or dropping her load.

He wasn't holding her arms tightly but she was strangely aware of each of his fingers as they wrapped warmly around her. Her pulse began to race as an extra surge of adrenaline flooded into her system but she was unable to drag her eyes away from him.

'Staff Nurse Pickering?' called a voice from somewhere a million miles away and the spell surrounding her was shattered.

'Y-yes, Sister,' she stammered, wrenching her gaze away. She tightened her grasp around the pile of linens and took a couple of shaky steps back so that he was finally forced to release his hold on her.

To her annoyance she still seemed to be able to feel the warmth of his hold on her arms several hours later when it was her turn to go to the canteen for her lunch break.

Confused by her juvenile preoccupation and annoyed that she'd found her eyes scanning every new person she met in case it was *him*, she made herself join a table full of nurses from other departments.

She had just made the conscious decision that if she was going to be able to keep her mind occupied she had to make an effort to join in with the usual round of gossip and chatter when she caught sight of him at a table on the other side of the room.

Once again she found herself unable to look away from him, but this time he was unaware of either her presence or her avid scrutiny, and she was far enough away to dare to take her time about looking at him.

Her pulse skipped when she saw that he was every bit as good looking as she remembered, his dark hair neat in spite of its tendency to curl and his face alert and intelligent as he spoke to his companion.

As she watched he gestured with one hand to emphasise a point, and she felt a sharp spiral of awareness when she remembered the gentle strength of those long fingers wrapped around her arms.

He laughed and she saw his teeth gleam whitely against the healthy tan of his face, his cheek-bones lean and angular under the harsh artificial lighting.

There'd been no time in their brief encounter for her to even glance at his identity tag. He could have been anyone from a student to a phlebotomist to a consultant.

Now that she saw him sitting with a colleague she could see a stethoscope stuffed in the overloaded pocket of his white coat and could read the word 'Obstetrics' on a small reference book tucked in behind it.

Remembering the direction from which he'd been coming, everything she'd heard on the ward this morning fell into place.

'Is that Dr Jones?' she interrupted to ask her closest neighbour with a shaky attempt at a nonchalant nod in his direction.

'Where?' her neighbour demanded, and openly stared around the rapidly filling room before she followed Livvy's gaze and spotted him at the table on the other side. 'Yes. That's him,' she confirmed with a feline purr of approval in her voice. 'Mr den Haag's new registrar. Totally gorgeous but totally unavailable.'

'What do you mean, unavailable? Is he married?' Livvy asked as her heart made a stupid dive towards the floor. For some reason she was unable to make the attempt at sounding casual even though there was no logical reason that the answer should matter to her one way or the other.

Even so, she was overcome by the irrational disappointment that she hadn't met him sooner—before he'd met his wife—because there was no way she could even contemplate a relationship with someone in his position. The idea of breaking up another's marriage was anathema to her, especially after the nightmare of her own father's infidelity and her parents' subsequent acrimonious divorce.

'Being married doesn't seem to stop *some* of the doctors tomcatting around,' her neighbour commented darkly, almost as if she had somehow picked up on Livvy's thoughts, 'but, no, he isn't married and isn't likely to be.'

'Why not? Is he homosexual?' Her eyes feasted on his lean good looks and mourned their loss to the gene pool if they were never to be passed on to his children.

'Good God! Gay?' her neighbour scoffed in disbelief. 'Does he look gay to you?'

Livvy watched him for a moment as he chatted and laughed with his male companion but there was nothing obvious in his body language to give her any clues as to his orientation.

'I've no idea,' Livvy said weakly as a measure of relief trickled through her. 'I haven't met enough to know.'

'Well, take it from me, he's far from it! But he's such a wary beast that I doubt anyone will ever entice *him* into the trap.'

The loud disbelief in her voice must have reached the other side of the room because as Livvy watched he glanced idly in the direction of their table. Suddenly his attention sharpened and she knew that he had recognised her.

It was an uncanny replay of the events in the corridor. As soon as his eyes met hers she was powerless to look away in spite of the fact there was the whole width of the busy room between them.

Livvy was oblivious to the movement of the others around her as they grumbled their way to their feet and set off back to their wards. All she could see was the pair of clear blue eyes, gazing at her with disturbing intensity while he sat clasping his forgotten cup between his hands.

His companion must have said something to break his concentration because for a few seconds he glanced away from her.

She was still sitting mesmerised by him when his eyes found her again, and her breathing stopped entirely when he stood and began to cross the room towards her.

'Daniel,' he said succinctly as he sat down in the seat opposite her, his eyes taking inventory of every feature before they returned to mesh with hers again.

'Livvy,' she whispered in reply, knowing somehow that was all the introduction necessary between them.

She was almost afraid of the intensity of the emotions overwhelming her. It couldn't be possible that he was touched by the same madness—not someone as wary as he was reputed to be—but he was equally silent and seemed equally strangely content just to be close.

'I'm sorry.'

As if someone had snapped their fingers, he suddenly switched his gaze from her face towards the latest group to come into the room and she saw the skin darken over his lean cheeks. 'It was very rude of me to stare at you like that.'

With a lift of her heart Livvy realised that he *was* feeling just as disconcerted by events as she was and she wanted to chuckle with delight. She'd never felt this sense of total connection with anyone in her life and knew that only total honesty would do.

'In which case, you'll have to accept *my* apologies, because I was staring, too,' she said quietly, and was helpless to stop her lips curving into a happy smile.

When he turned his blue gaze back to her she could see that her candour had surprised him, but then she saw understanding dawn and his answering smile begin in his eyes.

'Sister?'

A worried young voice dragged her away from memories of happier times and drew her eyes to the doorway to see the uncertain expression on the face of the young nurse standing there.

'I'm sorry to disturb you, Sister. I've helped Mrs Williams into a dry nightdress and made her comfortable but I think you need to come and have a look at her. And she said to tell you about Mrs Owens—that her contractions are only four minutes apart and she's beginning to get a bit anxious and—' She paused to gulp in a much-needed breath and Livvy held one hand up to stop the flow of words.

'In other words, all hell is breaking loose out there?' she asked with new purpose in her voice.

'Something like that, Sister,' the younger woman agreed with a nervous grin.

'Well, then, we'd better see if we can do something about sorting them all out.'

She glanced down at the empty case notes in her hand and held them out, glancing at the young woman's name badge as she handed them over.

'I'm sorry, Cherry, I don't recognise you but, then,

I've been away for a month. Have you worked on Maternity for long?' Livvy asked, wondering just how much help the rather nervous-looking youngster was going to be. If she was likely to fall apart at the slightest thing she wasn't going to last long on *this* ward, especially the way things were...

'This is my first week,' Cherry replied, her head coming up and her shoulders squaring in a very satisfactory way. 'I'm sorry if I seemed a bit of a wimp a minute or two ago but when I got to the office door just then, for one awful moment I thought you were in labour, too.'

There was still a trace of panic in her voice and Livvy couldn't help laughing.

'Don't get me wrong,' Cherry added in a hurry. 'I love the work up here and I've been coping well so far, but there are so few staff and so many patients and I'm so far off qualifying as a midwife that I know there's no way I'm ready to cope with a delivery on my own yet—especially a midwife's baby!'

Livvy laughed at her fervent addition.

'Well, Cherry, if we all keep our fingers crossed it won't come to that—but I can't promise! In the meantime, there's a new patient just getting settled into the bed with the curtains drawn. She's about three months pregnant and she's been in a car accident. Could you get her preliminary details before the technician comes up to do the ultrasound? She's a bit shaky so if you could take her a couple of cups of tea.'

'A couple?' Cherry queried in surprise.

'One for the shock and the other one to make sure her bladder's nice and full for a successful scan,' Livvy explained with a wicked smile, remembering the discomfort of it when she'd had her own scan.

She stood perfectly still for several seconds after the young nurse had set off on her task and massaged her aching back while she gathered her thoughts.

Yes, it had been a shock to be confronted by Daniel like that, but she couldn't afford to allow it to scramble her head. She might not be on duty *officially*, but over the next few hours she could end up with several women relying on her skill to help their precious babies out into the world. From now on she was going to concentrate on the job in hand. There would be plenty of time to mourn the loss of her love when he and his new wife were gone and *she* was back home in her own little cottage. This was no time to fall apart.

'Phone for Duncan French,' she muttered to herself as she leant forward to dial, not daring to sit down in case she couldn't get up again. 'I hope to goodness he's on his way...if the switchboard even remembered to page him. If Amy's busy upstairs then I'm going to need all the help I can get down here,' she continued under her breath as she waited for the call to connect.

A couple of minutes later she put the phone back down and, in spite of the danger of not wanting to stand up again, sank weakly onto the corner of the desk.

'I don't believe it!' she whispered, her voice rising to a squeak. 'I do *not* believe it!'

'What?' demanded a horribly familiar voice at the door, and she swivelled awkwardly to see Daniel enter the office.

It was like their first meeting all over again as her eyes were captured by the intensity of his and every rational thought disappeared under an avalanche of breathless attraction.

'What don't you believe?' he repeated, his dark brows

drawn into a frown, and just that suddenly the spell was broken.

'Not that it's any of your business, but I've just been told that the consultant had a fall on the ice in the car park this morning and he's got a Colles' fracture,' she retorted waspishly, needing to take her frustrations out on somebody. 'At this very moment he's in the plaster room, being immobilised up to his elbow.'

'Not Duncan French?'

'Yes, Duncan French,' she snapped, horribly conscious that she sounded rude and shrewish. 'He's the only consultant who matters at the moment.'

'Why did you need him? Are you having problems?' he demanded, his eyes flicking briefly to her own obvious pregnancy.

'Problems?' Livvy laughed shortly but it was a sound without humour as she raised one hand and began counting off on her fingers.

'*One*, it's snowing outside and we've got two wards full of full-term or ''at risk'' pregnant women who have been called into the hospital in case they go into labour while they're cut off by snow.

'*Two*, it's Christmas Eve and we're down to the bare minimum of staff because of a flu epidemic.

'*Three*, there are two women upstairs in Obs and Gynae in the early stages of labour with a midwife who is in the throes of morning sickness.

'*Four*, there's one woman down here on Maternity hooked up to a foetal monitor and two in labour, one with her waters already broken.

'*Five*, a few minutes ago we had another woman arrive in advanced labour. She's a visitor to the area and until the antenatal notes from her own hospital get here we'll be working blind. She's had to go upstairs because there isn't anywhere else for her to go.

'And then there's your...' She paused, unable to force the word 'wife' past her lips. How could she think of the other woman as Daniel's wife when, until just a few moments ago, she had believed that *she* was still married to him.

She started again.

'*Six*, there's the victim of the car crash, waiting for the technician to arrive to do an ultrasound scan to check that the baby's all right.'

'What about the registrar?' he demanded, and she could see from the familiar intent expression on his face that he was already assimilating everything she'd told him and was cataloguing the priorities and implications. 'We saw him in Casualty not long ago when he was called down to look at Alice. Won't he be coming straight back up here?'

'He probably did, unless Casualty had another patient for him to see.'

'Well, then...?' He paused expectantly.

'He's having to spread himself very thinly at the moment, and they won't all fit in the delivery suite at once,' Livvy explained with dwindling patience. 'Apart from that, he's already been on duty for twelve hours and the poor beggar's only just getting over his own bout of flu. He shouldn't really be back on duty yet.'

He gave a nod as if everything was now clear and his chin lifted in the way that told her that, having absorbed all the data, he had come to a decision.

'In that case,' he announced briskly, 'it looks as if it was your good luck that our accident happened in your catchment area because you just acquired another pair of hands.'

'We...what?' He couldn't be saying what it sounded like. Was Daniel suggesting that he stepped into Duncan French's shoes during the emergency?

She should be delighted that they were acquiring the services of such a well-qualified doctor in their hour of need, but all she was aware of was the way her heart sank.

Surely, after all her efforts to remove herself from the heartbreak of his presence, she wasn't going to end up working beside him again, the way they'd worked together at St Augustine's? That might be just too much to bear in her present fragile emotional state.

'I read a piece of research that suggested that women's brains shrank during pregnancy,' Daniel commented pointedly, breaking into her thoughts. 'I discounted the theory at first, but you could make me reconsider. You weren't this slow on the uptake before. What do you *think* I meant? You're short of senior staff in the department and, apparently, in the middle of a minor population explosion. It should be obvious that I'm offering to pitch in and help.'

Just the thought of spending the next few hours working with him was enough to short-circuit her brain so she concentrated on his inflammatory comment.

'I've always thought that women's brains shrink *before* they get pregnant or they'd never put themselves through it,' she retorted sharply, taking the brake off her tongue as she glared up at him.

Her pithy reply made one corner of his mouth lift in a familiar lopsided grin before his eyes fell to the evidence of her own pregnancy and all humour fled.

For just a second she thought she recognised pain in his eyes as he visibly gauged how far along her condition had progressed, then they darkened. Again, a complex mixture of expressions followed each other across his face and again she thought she recognised pain amid anger, frustration, suspicion and disappointment.

She knew he wanted to ask questions and knew he was going to demand answers but she also knew she wasn't ready to give them to him—not while her emotions were still so much in turmoil.

Knowing it was cowardly to run away from the situation, she turned towards the door before he could frame his first words.

'I'll send someone to find you a white coat,' she began, hoping to sound brisk and efficient but aware that she more than likely sounded as if she was gabbling in her hurry to escape. 'Then, if you would like to join me out in the ward, I'll be checking up on the patients.'

She reached the open doorway and was taking her first shaky breath of relief when his voice reached her.

'Olivia.'

It was just her name, but spoken just that way in his unmistakably husky voice it was enough to stop her in her tracks.

She reached out one hand to grasp the wooden frame as her knees turned to silly putty, not daring to do any more than turn her head to look over her shoulder at him.

'Sooner or later, we need to talk,' he said softly into the silent room behind her.

Livvy nodded just once, knowing he was right.

He needed to know that she wasn't going to try to make trouble between him and his new wife, especially while the distressed woman's pregnancy might be at risk.

She wasn't happy about the way her own marriage to Daniel had ended, but after what she'd seen in her own parents' marriage she'd always believed that a man couldn't be 'stolen' unless he wanted to be.

Daniel's marriage today made it obvious what his choice had been.

But while her pride insisted that she should concentrate on walking away from him calmly and firmly she couldn't quite subdue the little voice inside that was trying to warn her that his words could have equally been a simple statement or a veiled threat.

Thank goodness she was going to be too busy to think for the foreseeable future, Livvy thought wryly as she worked her way systematically round the ward again.

She'd never understood why one woman going into labour seemed to trigger others into following suit, but the phenomenon was certainly in full force at the moment, both here and upstairs.

'Well, Megan, how's it going?' Livvy asked as she perched one hip on the edge of the bed. The tinsel wound around the frame of the headboard shimmered with the movement, sending coloured flashes across the wall to join the rest of the festive decoration, but her patient was quite oblivious.

She'd had a feeling that things had started progressing when the older woman had given up marching up and down the ward between contractions and had opted to make herself comfortable instead.

'It's just about reached the moment where I'm ready to castrate my husband if he even *thinks* of coming near me again,' she muttered through gritted teeth, her eyes squeezed tightly closed as she tried to block her surroundings out and concentrate.

Livvy waited for the contraction to ease, one hand gently resting on the bowling-ball hardness of the woman's belly while she tracked its progress.

'I must be mad!' Megan panted when the pain's grip eased slightly. 'What on earth could ever make this agony worthwhile?'

'Oh, I don't know,' Livvy mused aloud, taking the rhetorical question literally. 'Probably that very first second you get to hold your new baby and count all the fingers and toes.'

Megan chuckled weakly and ran shaky fingers through her limp hair to take it off her sweaty face.

'You're right, dammit, but just at this moment I wish you weren't, especially when I know I've still got a lot of this to go through. It would be nice to put all the blame on someone else— then I could suggest they went through this for me, too!'

'Do you need anything for the pain?' Livvy offered, not wanting to see anyone suffer unnecessarily.

'It's not too bad at the moment,' Meagan answered stoically, accepting a sip of water with a grateful smile. 'I'd rather wait until a bit later when I'll really need something.'

Livvy sat with her for a few minutes longer, glad of the chance to rest while she unobtrusively timed the interval between Megan's contractions. Her own backache seemed to have gone away for the moment so she was being careful to pace herself in the hope that it wouldn't return.

'It might not take quite as long as you think,' she suggested, glancing at her watch again when a groan announced the speedy onset of the next one. 'You're progressing quite quickly now.'

Megan pulled a face in reply, obviously not wanting to interrupt her quietly controlled breathing as she rode out the pain.

Livvy heard the phone ring at the other end of the ward and glanced across, glad to see Pat Lersh hurry to answer it so she could keep Megan company a little longer.

A beckoning hand told her that her rest break was over.

'I'm needed at the other end for a minute,' she said as she forced herself to straighten again and tugged on the hem of her smock. Her back twinged briefly, the pain spreading in a broad band across the top of her hips, but it was soon gone. 'Don't forget, if you need anything press your call button or just give a shout.'

Megan gave her a silent thumbs-up sign and closed her eyes to concentrate on her breathing again.

'It's Amy,' Pat said as she passed the phone over.

'Ringing to gloat that you've delivered your first one already?' Livvy demanded as soon as she was connected.

'Hardly!' said Amy. 'Just the opposite, in fact. It's that visitor. I think we've got a big problem here. From what she says, she's carrying twins but it feels like a couple of octopuses with neither head engaged. Has the technician finished doing the ultrasound on your accident victim yet? I need to see what's happening in there.'

'I don't know,' Livvy admitted, but didn't tell Amy that she'd actually been avoiding looking towards the newest patient in the ward. There was no way she

wanted to see any more of Daniel and Alice Jones together than she had to.

'Can you find out and let me know?' Amy asked, her
voice sounding a little frazzled. 'Or, better yet, send the
equipment along as soon as you can—before yours is
done, if possible.'

Livvy felt a little guilty that she hadn't followed up
on the arrival of the ultrasound technician, knowing that
it was her own personal problems that had prompted the
neglect.

'Your patient definitely takes priority over mine,' she
said briskly. 'I'll check to see where the equipment's got
to and send it straight along. If not, I'll phone you with
an update.'

She cradled the phone and began to run her finger
down the list of numbers to find the right one. Absent-
mindedly she began to massage the niggling ache that
had appeared in her back again, hoping that it would
disappear again as quickly as it had earlier.

There was far too much to do for her to be able to
afford to waste any time on her own health, she thought
as she found the number she was looking for and began
to tap it out. The patients definitely had to come first
and, as with triage in the casualty department, the most
urgent cases needed attention first, no matter who they
were or who they had married...

'What equipment is that?' demanded a husky tenor
voice right behind her, startling her so much she nearly
dropped the phone.

Livvy whirled as fast as her awkward shape permitted
to face its owner, her pulse suddenly racing.

# CHAPTER THREE

'You made me jump!' Livvy exclaimed breathlessly, before turning back to complete her call. She felt marginally less vulnerable in Daniel's presence if she wasn't actually facing him.

'Which equipment were you talking about?' he repeated. 'The ultrasound?'

'Yes. I need to find out where it's— Ah! Dewi? This is Sister Jones up on Maternity. When do you expect to reach us?'

She listened to the slightly rambling reply, finding it hard to keep her mind on what she was hearing when every nerve seemed to be concentrating on the fact that Daniel was right behind her.

The technician was full of apologies for not arriving sooner, and Livvy could clearly picture the painfully slender young woman as soon as she heard her distinctive Indonesian accent.

It was a relief, in a way, to have to focus on the fractured English rather than let her attention wander to the fact that her nose was telling her that Daniel was still using the same soap and shampoo he had when they were married.

It would be disastrous if she were to allow herself to think about how familiar it felt to have him standing so close that she was surrounded by the same indefinable mixture of warmth, soap and man that would forever be Daniel.

'So, you're free to come up straight away?' Livvy questioned at last, dragging her attention back to the matter in hand.

'Good,' muttered a masculine voice behind her. 'About time...'

Livvy turned to glare at him and found he was even closer than she'd thought. She drew in a hasty breath to combat the strange light-headed feeling that attacked her and continued what she was saying.

'Don't bother coming here,' she directed briskly. 'Go straight upstairs to—'

'What? No!' he exclaimed sharply, one hand coming out in a silent demand for the receiver.

Undeterred, Livvy half turned away from him so that the phone was out of his reach and continued.

'Sister Aldarini is waiting for you to arrive so if you could get there as soon as possible.'

She paused just long enough for the technician to confirm her instructions then hung up.

'How dare you?' Daniel said, his deadly quiet voice more potent than any shout. 'There's a woman out there in that ward who's still shocked by a car crash and is worried sick that she's in danger of losing her baby. It wouldn't have taken long for the technician to set her mind at rest—or was that why you chose to do it?'

For a moment Livvy was speechless that he could believe her capable of such contemptible pettiness.

God knew she had little enough reason to like the woman, but for Daniel to accuse her of deliberately delaying a test that could set Alice's mind at rest only showed how little he respected her.

She swallowed the bile that rose in the back of her throat and concentrated on the facts.

'No, it wouldn't take very long,' Livvy agreed with a hard-won appearance of control, 'but, either way, even you would have to admit that having the ultrasound half an hour earlier or later won't make any difference to the outcome.'

She clenched her fists, feeling her short nails score the soft skin of her palms as she fixed him with a furious gaze and saw him frown darkly, his blue eyes flashing like steel. He would have interrupted if she hadn't continued heatedly.

'Unfortunately, while *she* just needs to have a little peace of mind, there's a woman upstairs, carrying twins who's already in labour with neither baby engaged, and as her antenatal clinic notes *still* haven't arrived from her own hospital I assumed her case would be *slightly* more urgent.'

There was an awful silence when she'd finished speaking, and as the open sarcasm in her voice echoed and re-echoed inside her head Livvy suddenly wondered if she had gone too far.

It was one thing to defend her decision with carefully reasoned facts, but it was another thing entirely to berate a doctor with such venom.

'You're absolutely right,' Daniel said quietly. 'I had no right to criticise your actions without asking for an explanation.'

Instantly, Livvy was speechless again and very close to tears.

This was the Daniel she had fallen in love with—an honest man incapable of duplicity, a man who wasn't afraid to admit to a mistake or make an apology if he found himself in the wrong.

What had happened to change him? They had been

so happy until the older woman had come into their lives. What had been the attraction? What hold had Alice Webster had over him that he would break his solemn promises to Livvy?

'Amy will send it straight down as soon as they've finished scanning the mum upstairs,' she finally managed through the tears thickening her throat, using the pain of her nails still embedded in her palms to maintain some semblance of calm. 'In the meantime, I think it might be a good idea if you went along to the delivery room in case the poor woman needs surgical intervention.'

He nodded soberly then one eyebrow lifted in his own familiar way.

'Don't tell me that this is one of your "feelings",' he teased quietly. 'When we worked together at St Augustine's I came to dread the times you started a sentence with "I think it might be a good idea if you…". It usually meant that there was a complication about to happen.'

Livvy pulled a face.

'I can't help it,' she protested. 'When Amy said it felt like two octopuses I had a sudden mental image of how difficult it was going to be to untangle the two of them between contractions and still end up with two healthy babies.'

'As usual, I will bow to your intuition,' he said with a quickly sketched salute. 'If she does need help it's better to do it before all three of them are in distress.'

'Good luck,' she murmured as he turned towards the door, a sudden flood of memories of all the difficult cases he'd successfully rescued briefly softening her attitude towards the new Mrs Jones. 'Shall I explain to…to

Alice why there's been a delay?' With the best will in the world, she couldn't force herself to call the woman his wife.

'That would help to set her mind at rest,' he accepted. 'We still haven't heard how my father's doing in surgery so it would be one less pressure.'

'Your father? In surgery?' Livvy parroted, aghast. 'What's the matter with him?'

She'd really liked her former father-in-law and had admired the way he had steadfastly loved and cared for his severely disabled wife.

The last time she'd seen him had been several months after the poor woman's death when he'd still been struggling with very mixed emotions. She'd known that he'd been consumed with grief that he'd lost her and that he'd felt guilty for his relief that her suffering was finally over, but she'd always believed that there'd been something more, eating away at his soul.

She'd always thought that he would have loved to have had a large brood of children instead of a single son, and had hoped her marriage to Daniel would provide him with several grandchildren to spoil to his heart's content.

Unfortunately, it was just hours after she found out that the first of those children might be on the way that she had also found out about Alice Webster. Livvy had confronted him, but when Daniel had refused to tell her what had been going on between himself and the older woman their marriage had fallen apart.

'My father was injured in the accident,' Daniel was saying, dragging her attention back to the present day. 'The car hit a patch of black ice hidden under the snow and spun out of control. His side of the car took the impact when it slammed broadside into a lamppost. Orthopaedics are trying to put his hip and thigh back together but I've no idea yet how successful they're going to be.'

Livvy cringed. She wanted to express her sadness that the kindly man had been injured, particularly when it had happened on what should have been such a special day, but before she could speak the phone rang.

'Sister Jones,' Livvy said promptly, and frowned when she heard Amy's voice on the other end.

'It's a hopeless malpresentation,' she heard her colleague say rapidly, barely taking the time to introduce herself.

'The two of them look almost as if they're lying across each other, belly-to-belly, with their arms and legs wrapped around each other. The one closest to the vagina is lying transverse so the other one can't present for delivery.

'There's no way we're going to be able to deliver them normally, I can't find Aled anywhere and there's no room in Theatre even though I have managed to find an anaesthetist still on his feet.'

From the sound of it, this was the sort of case that could go wrong in a hurry—the sort of situation that could cause nightmares—but Livvy had no doubt that Daniel could deal with it.

She covered the mouthpiece just long enough to relay the information to Daniel and, as she had anticipated, he swiftly agreed with her feeling that surgical intervention was probably the only viable option.

'Amy?' she said, returning to the call. 'Get everything prepped and ready because help will be with you in about two minutes.'

'Two minutes?' squeaked Amy in disbelief. 'In that case, Superman must have just flown in because I know Duncan French isn't fit for duty and they haven't been able to get hold of anyone else.'

'Not quite Superman, but near enough,' Livvy joked with a grin. 'Now get on with it because when he gets there to look at the ultrasound he won't want to hang about.'

She put the phone down and turned to Daniel.

'She's got the anaesthetist standing by and the technician's there with the ultrasound. Is there anything else I can tell you?'

'Well, I'm disappointed to hear that you don't believe I'm Superman,' he joked, then continued more seriously, 'But I knew that your intuition about an impending problem was probably right on target so I'm not surprised. Just for the sake of argument, tell me what you think.'

'It sounds to me as if you're going to have to do a Caesarean in the delivery room,' Livvy said succinctly, subduing the leap of pleasure his words of praise had caused. 'With the ultrasound showing one twin lying transverse so neither of them can be delivered normally, you haven't really got any option, and there isn't time to wait to transfer them up to Theatre even if there was one free.'

'As I said, that intuition of yours...' He allowed the sentence to die away with a wry smile. 'You'd better point me in the right direction so I can scrub up.'

'Better than that, I'll show you,' Livvy said, leading the way out of the office. 'I'm probably going to be involved in another delivery by the time you're free to come back and I need the ladies' room before I can contemplate that. Anyway,' she added honestly, 'I'd like a quick look at that ultrasound myself. If I remember rightly, the presentation Amy described only happens in about five per cent of deliveries involving twins.'

By the time Livvy had made a detour to tell the new Mrs Jones the bare bones of why her ultrasound would be a little delayed, and had made herself comfortable, Daniel had scrubbed up and was gowned and gloved and ready to start.

'Let's see what you've got,' he prompted, and Amy recited the latest observations of each of her three patients while Dewi ran the ultrasound again.

There was silence for several moments while he concentrated fiercely on the shadowy outlines, obviously making certain that he had the babies' internal geography right before he started.

'Please, Doctor, are my babies all right?' whispered the patient when he turned towards her again, her pale, terrified face gleaming with perspiration under the bright lights as she hung onto her husband's hand.

'Mrs Simpson, from what I can see, your two look absolutely perfect. The only problem is that you've already taught them such good manners that each one is saying, "After you," "No, after you," and neither wants to be first out into the world.'

The young woman couldn't help a giggle of relief at his nonsense and she glanced up at her husband.

'We both wanted to see them being born, but now it looks as if we're going to miss it.'

'I'm afraid there isn't time to give you an epidural to allow you to be awake for the delivery, not without risking the babies—'

'No,' her husband interrupted fiercely. 'We're not going to do anything to risk harming the babies. God willing, we'll have them for the rest of their lives, so the first few minutes aren't that important.'

'What he means,' his wife butted in before Daniel could comment, 'is that he's terrified that he'll pass out if he sees any of the gory stuff.'

Livvy saw the look of male understanding Daniel exchanged with the bashful father-to-be.

'I know what you mean,' Daniel said with a grimace. 'This childbirth stuff isn't nearly as interesting for us men as starting the babies off.'

'Well, we can both enjoy that bit,' Mr Simpson agreed. He got an embarrassed dig in his ribs from his wife but it didn't stop him from continuing. 'I just don't like the idea that Jill's going to go through such pain and I can't do anything for her, and as for cutting her up—'

'I've got a suggestion,' Daniel said, butting in before he could go into any more graphic description. 'I know your wife isn't going to be able to be awake for the babies to be born, but if we rig up a screen so you can't see the grisly bits you could sit up by her head. Then we can pass you each of the babies as soon as they're born so you can tell her all about them when she wakes up.'

Mr Simpson looked doubtful but his wife had a newly hopeful expression in spite of the fact that another painful contraction was starting. Livvy could see that she was willing her husband to agree to Daniel's plan.

'You're sure I wouldn't see anything gory if I stay here with her?' the young man demanded, obviously needing reassurance.

'Scout's honour,' Daniel promised, raising one gloved hand, and the deal was struck.

Livvy would have loved to have stayed to watch
Daniel operate the way she had when they'd worked
together at St Augustine's. She remembered only too
clearly how exciting it had been to work with someone
of his expertise, but there were other patients back on
the ward she had to supervise.

With a cheerful wave and good wishes she left the
room, glancing back briefly through the window to see
Daniel's face settle into familiar lines of concentration
as he signalled the anaesthetist to begin.

'Sister. Thank God you're back,' Pat Lersh said fervently almost before the doors had swung closed behind
her. 'I just rang through to find you and they told me
you were on your way. Mrs Williams's baby suddenly
seems to be in a hurry to arrive.'

Livvy changed direction and made straight for
Megan's bed.

'Staff Nurse says you're trying to catch us on the
hop,' she said cheerfully as she reached her bedside.'

'I don't know about that, but things certainly seem to
have speeded up in the last ten minutes,' she agreed. 'I'd
be delighted, except no one seems to know where to find
my husband. He's always been at work when I've gone
into labour with the other babies and he's missed every
one of them coming. This time, because he's already at
the hospital, I thought he'd be able to see one of them
born—especially as it might be his last chance.'

The last pointed words were forced out through gritted
teeth as the next contraction took vicious hold of her.

Livvy spoke calmingly to her until the pain began to
fade, telling her that they would transfer her to the labour

suite as soon as she caught her breath, but barely had that contraction eased than it was replaced almost immediately by the next one. Things had certainly been moving quickly since she'd gone up to the delivery room to have a look at Mrs Simpson's ultrasound.

'I want to push,' Megan gasped desperately. 'Is it time yet or will I hurt the baby?'

'Don't push until I've had a chance to check you inside,' Livvy ordered as she hurriedly pulled the curtains around to give some semblance of privacy. It didn't look as if there was going to be time to move Megan out of the ward before this little one arrived in the world. 'I must make certain that you're fully dilated or you could damage yourself inside so pant like a dog during your contraction.'

Livvy turned to ask Pat Lersh to fetch a sterile obstetric tray but the staff nurse had obviously anticipated the request and was already standing there with one in her hands.

'Well done,' Livvy murmured as she broke the seals on the package and carefully unfolded it so that she only touched the outside. 'Could you pour the povidone-iodine scrub over my hands...?'

With a speed born of long practice, Livvy thoroughly cleaned her hands. They all chuckled when she donned the sterile apron, which had no chance of reaching around her waist, but it was more important that she pulled on the gloves supplied in the tray.

'If you can raise your hips for a moment,' she prompted, and slid a sterile towel underneath, without touching either her patient or the bedclothes.

She draped a second towel flat across the bed under

Megan's thighs and draped sterile cloths over her abdomen and each thigh.

'Now we just need to find Mr Williams or he's going to miss the show.'

'Again,' Megan Williams panted. 'Could someone check the smokers' lounge to see if he's there? He gave up a couple of years ago when our last one was born, but if the other dads are smoking...' She ran out of breath, wincing as Livvy began her examination.

'All right, Megan,' Livvy said as she straightened, hoping that the twinges in her own back would ease before she had to do anything more involved than examine her patient. 'Everything's fine in there so next time you get a contraction you can start pushing.'

'You mean now?' the older woman joked wryly on a quick gasp of breath before she closed her eyes tightly and bore down.

Matters seemed to move very quickly after that and the baby's head was already crowning when there was the sound of hurrying footsteps approaching the curtain.

'Can I come in?' said a male voice in a harsh whisper, and Livvy suddenly realised how quiet the ward was. Someone must have turned the video off because she couldn't hear the soundtrack of *Pride and Prejudice* playing any more. There was just the sound of Christmas carols, drifting in from somewhere along the corridor.

'Of course you can come in, you daft beggar,' muttered his wife. 'Better late than never.'

'Am I too late, then?' he demanded, disappointment clear in his voice as he fought his way through the curtains, while trying to shove beefy arms into a gown and tie on a mask at the same time.

'Just in time,' Livvy reassured him, and directed him

to the other side of the bed. 'If you sit beside Megan you can hold her hand.'

He sidled around the end of the bed and Livvy saw him glance tentatively towards his wife and do a double-take.

'Hell, love, I can see the head!' he exclaimed, then blushed furiously. 'Sorry for swearing, Sister,' he muttered, and slunk into the chair.

'Don't worry about it,' she said with a grin. 'The baby isn't far enough out yet to hear you.'

Megan gave a snort of laughter but it was cut off by the start of the next contraction.

'Earn your keep,' she muttered as she groped for her husband's hand and squeezed it tightly.

Within minutes the head was delivered and after a few seconds' pause—while Livvy checked that the cord wasn't around the baby's neck—it took just one more sustained push for the shoulders to appear and the slippery bundle slid out into Livvy's hands, already objecting noisily.

'It's another boy!' exclaimed Mr Williams in awe as he caught his first glimpse of the squirming infant.

Livvy chuckled heartily.

'I think you're boasting again,' she teased as she moved aside the thick umbilical cord draped between the baby's legs and revealed the distinct lack of male appendages. 'You've got a daughter.'

'At last!' Megan breathed, a beatific smile flooding her face as Livvy lay the baby across her stomach to check the baby over and take care of the cord. 'I'll have someone to take *my* side in family arguments for a change.'

Livvy knew that Meagan had three boys already and

that the most important consideration was that the baby should arrive healthy, but she also knew how much Megan had been hoping that this one would be the little girl she'd yearned for.

After making sure that the baby's airways were clear and totting up an excellent Apgar score, it was a real delight to wrap her in a towel and give the proud new parents a few minutes to savour their delight.

Megan automatically offered the infant her breast and the picture of contentment was complete.

'Shall I take Dad to get his new daughter cleaned and dressed while you take care of Mum?' Pat offered behind Livvy when she saw her finish recording the time of birth and the five-minute Apgar score.

'If Megan can bear to let go of her,' she teased, her eyes pricking as she saw the utter delight in the way Megan was examining the miniature perfection of each tiny finger and toe.

It was a very proud father who gingerly scooped his baby daughter up, then settled her comfortably into the crook of his arm before he made his way towards the opening in the curtain.

When he emerged into the ward there was a spontaneous round of applause and various shouts of congratulations from the rest of the patients and their visitors.

'Anyone would think *he'd* done all the hard work,' Megan grumbled as renewed contractions heralded the expulsion of the placenta, but Livvy could see from the smile on her face that she was far too overjoyed for it to be anything more than a token complaint.

'It's certainly the most public delivery I've done so far,' Livvy said, as she massaged the flaccid abdomen gently over the fundus to help the expulsion of the afterbirth. 'I wasn't aware of it at the time, but the rest of the ward must have been able to hear every word in here.'

'My God!' Megan whispered, looking stricken, her concentration completely diverted from what Livvy was doing. 'Did I use a lot of bad language?'

'Not a bit of it, in spite of the fact you didn't want any pain relief,' Livvy assured her with a grin as she finished tidying everything away and made her patient comfortable. She'd been delighted to confirm that Megan hadn't torn at all. 'The whole thing happened so quickly and, anyway, you didn't have any breath to spare for swearing.'

'You're not joking. This was the quickest of any of the babies. If you could guarantee that they'd all be this easy, I wouldn't mind having a few more.'

'You're talking about having more of them already?' demanded her husband, as he carried their new daughter through the curtains, this time wrapped in a soft pink blanket. 'Just over an hour ago you were threatening to dock my tail if I came anywhere near you. That's why I ran away to hide!'

'I'd only want another one if I could be sure it would be another girl,' Megan pointed out, her arms already reaching for her precious daughter. 'They seem to be much easier to give birth to than the boys were and it would help to even up the teams at home.'

Her work finished for the time being, Livvy offered the two of them the option of leaving the curtains closed.

'I'd rather show her off,' Megan said with a happy grin so Livvy drew the curtains back and carried the debris away, leaving the two of them to field all the comments from the surrounding beds as they admired their new treasure.

More than one of the mums-in-waiting voiced their jealousy that Megan's waiting was over, but a quick glance to one side as she walked the length of the ward reminded Livvy that not everyone was thinking similarly.

In spite of her personal animosity towards the woman, she couldn't help feeling a twinge of sympathy for the new Mrs Jones as she lay waiting to find out whether the fragile life inside her was going to survive.

'It must be so hard for her, listening to all this, while her own baby's at risk of dying,' she murmured to Pat Lersh as she finished writing up her notes on the delivery. 'If the whole department wasn't in such uproar she wouldn't have to be in here with mums and babies.'

'It will be even worse if she does lose it and still has to stay in here,' Pat said quietly. 'We'll just have to cross our fingers for her.'

The phone warbled and Livvy went to reach out for it, but her arm just wasn't long enough from that side of the desk with her prominent bulge in the way.

'If you went on a diet I'm sure it wouldn't take you long to get rid of that fat you've accumulated around your waist,' Pat teased as she lifted the receiver and passed it across.

'Cheek!' Livvy complained before she put it to her ear.

'Two boys,' announced Daniel without preamble. The husky tenor sounded like rich brown velvet and she could sense his smile of delight even over the phone. 'Mother and babies doing well.'

'And Father?' Livvy prompted, remembering how nervous the poor man had been.

'Coped beautifully,' Daniel confirmed. 'We've even chased a camera up and managed to get a photo of him, holding the two of them. He hasn't stopped smiling yet.'

'Well, we haven't been idle in your absence,' Livvy pointed out. 'Mrs Williams is now the proud possessor of a little daughter.'

'Wonderful. Tell her I'll be in to see her as soon as I can. I want to wait with Mrs Simpson until she comes out of the anaesthetic so I can set her mind at rest about the operation.'

'How long before you want to move her back to a ward—only I've been wondering whether it might be better to have all the post-delivery mums in the same place?' Livvy asked, mentally planning how many beds they would have to move.

'She can stay here for a bit of peace and quiet until the room's needed for the next delivery, but unless there are any particular problems, having the two wards mixed, I think it would be better to leave well enough alone. The mums in labour have collected their own cheering squads around them and it seems to be creating a good atmosphere.'

Livvy had to agree with him. They could always review the situation later if necessary. Everything seemed to be happening in a topsy-turvy fashion today.

Ideally, when Megan had been ready to deliver, she should have been moved into the specially equipped room so that everything would have been ready to hand if an emergency had developed, but the second stage of her labour had happened so fast she'd been lucky that there had been time to draw the curtains around.

Livvy was hardly surprised when she looked at the watch pinned to the front of her uniform and realised that she'd missed out on mid-morning teas and coffees. The morning had been so full of activity that it seemed as if hours had passed.

'I don't think I've ever seen an atmosphere like it,' Pat commented, as she grabbed a couple of biscuits and settled herself on the corner of the desk with the large mug of coffee she'd made to keep Livvy company. 'The whole ward is buzzing with adrenaline.'

'Well, you must admit, it has been an exciting morning,' said Cherry, her eyes shining. 'I never realised that things could be so dramatic. I thought it took hours and hours of waiting around for the contractions to finish doing their job, and then ages more while the mum slowly pushed the baby into the world.'

'Well, you've learnt an important lesson, then,' Daniel said as he walked into the room, the sound of his voice shocking Livvy's pulse into double speed. 'With pregnant mums, you always have to expect the unexpected.'

'A couple of the men looked a bit green around the gills when they realised they were going to be eavesdropping on the birth,' Pat commented with a grin.

Livvy was following the conversation with half of her attention while her eyes followed Daniel as he poured himself a drink and turned to lean easily against the edge of the desk. As she watched, he casually crossed his long legs at the ankles and wrapped his free arm around his lean waist to provide a prop for the other elbow.

'It's one thing to see a sanitised video of edited highlights of a birth at the antenatal classes with a midwife explaining everything,' he commented with a grin.

'Their imaginations must have been doing overtime this morning when they only had the soundtrack running.'

Livvy joined in the laughter. She'd been too busy, concentrating on the job in hand, at the time to think about the other people surrounding them and what they would be hearing.

'You should have seen the grin on Mr Williams's face when everybody applauded,' Cherry added. 'He looked proud enough to burst.'

'By the look of things, we're going to be seeing quite a bit of that look around today, with the number of women already in labour upstairs and down here,' Daniel said as he ran his fingers through his hair and absently ruffled the dark strands.

Livvy recognised the unconscious gesture and only just managed to hide a bittersweet smile behind her coffee-mug.

Soon after their first meeting she'd noticed that whenever he'd taken off one of those dreadful 'paper knickers' hats after an operation he'd always had to lift his hair off his head where it had been flattened.

So many little mannerisms she remembered from their time together, so many little things that tugged at her heartstrings.

Most of all, she'd always loved his open delight when he'd been able to hand a healthy new baby to its mother, and had daydreamed about the time when it would be his own child he was holding—*their* child.

Livvy rested her hand on top of the pronounced bulge of her advanced pregnancy and tried to subdue the sudden surge of sadness.

The last couple of hours had brought back some of her pleasure in working with the man who used to be her husband. It was hard to make herself remember that he had a new wife now and she was still waiting for the ultrasound to confirm the safety of her second pregnancy. That was absolute confirmation that the best of her dreams would never come true.

She'd had no idea what had been ahead of her when he'd asked her to marry him. She'd believed that he had meant the promises they'd made to each other, that he'd been an honest man who would have kept his word.

Where had her famous intuition been then?

# CHAPTER FOUR

'WILL you marry me?'

Livvy's heart leapt when she heard the husky words. She had never dreamt that Daniel was going to ask her, not when they'd known each other for such a short time.

'Oh, Daniel,' she breathed, as she looked at him across the secluded restaurant table, knowing that her feelings for him must be displayed on her face. 'Are you sure?'

'I was sure the first time I met you,' he murmured, his voice strangely fervent as he leaned closer so that only she could hear his words. He caught her hand and held it between his and she felt surrounded by his lean strength and infused with his confidence until she was certain she was invincible and dared to reveal her own feelings.

'I felt as if I'd found the other half of myself,' she admitted. 'Being with you felt so right that it seemed as if we must have known each other for years.'

And it *still* felt like that weeks later, with the certainty that he was the only man for her growing with every day.

From that first collision in the corridor to the meeting in the staff dining room and every time they'd been to- gether since, it was as if there was a special connection between them. For the first time in her life she knew she had met someone she could trust with her heart and soul.

'Yes, Daniel, I'd be delighted to marry you,' she said, and happiness burst into full bloom inside her.

'When?' he demanded, and the hint of relief she detected in his voice told her that until she'd answered he hadn't been absolutely certain that she'd accept.

'When do you think would be best? In the summer?' she suggested, suddenly imagining Daniel standing tall beside her as she wore a traditional flowing white dress. In her mind, the two of them were surrounded by sunshine and flowers and happy laughter.

'In the summer?' he echoed hollowly, his straight brows creasing into a troubled frown. 'That's months away. Why so long? Are you having second thoughts? Or are you afraid you're going to have them?'

'No. Not at all. I just thought… Well, it would give us time to get everything organised and make decisions about where we're going to live and…' When she realised that her explanation hadn't changed his expression she ground to a halt and turned the tables. 'When did you have in mind?'

'Saturday,' he said, without a second's hesitation.

'*Saturday?* But…but, it's Tuesday today, and…' She was so stunned her brain refused to form the words to tell him how impossible his suggestion was.

Daniel didn't have that problem as he hurried into details. 'You could go out tomorrow to find a dress while I book a room at one of the local hotels for a celebration meal with our friends. Then we'll have two days free to pack your things up and move them to my flat ready for Saturday. What else needs doing?'

'Well…' Livvy was completely at a loss and her thoughts were whirling around in her head far too fast for her to catch any of them and examine them closely.

Why was he trying to arrange everything so quickly?

This was going to be one of the most important days of their lives. Didn't he want to take the time to get everything perfect?

They'd never even mentioned the topic of marriage before so she had no idea about his feelings on the subject. Perhaps he didn't feel the same way as she did about the solemnity of the step they were contemplating. Perhaps, in this divorce-prone society, he saw it as a fairly temporary situation and not worth a great deal of fuss…

'Olivia?' The way his husky voice sounded when he said her name always sent a shiver up her spine, and she tried to shove all her misgivings to the back of her mind as she met his intent gaze.

'Why do you want to get married so soon?' she challenged softly, mindful that they were surrounded by other diners in the softly lit room.

'Because I love you and don't want to wait any longer than we have to,' he said, his blunt words sending a thrill right to her core. She would defy any woman to hear those fervent words, without melting.

It wasn't just the words that affected her, though, but the utter conviction in his eyes and on his face.

'You mean, you don't want to wait because you want to become more…intimate? Is it because we haven't… haven't slept together?' she asked, remembering snippets of articles she'd read in magazines from time to time.

The two of them hadn't made love yet, but their kisses and caresses had been growing ever more passionate so that sometimes it had been hard to draw back from the brink.

Was it true that men couldn't survive very long without the physical release of sex? To her knowledge, gleaned from the highly efficient hospital grapevine, in all the time he had been working at St Augustine's Daniel had avoided any relationship that might have ended up in bed.

Silently she berated her own ignorance of such matters.

What did she know about the needs of a virile man such as Daniel? Perhaps if she'd bothered to accept more invitations during her teens and early twenties she wouldn't be left, wandering about in the dark like this.

'We haven't slept together, but we haven't slept apart either,' he said, one corner of his mouth curving up wryly. 'At least *I* haven't slept. Not since I met you. I just lie there, thinking about you. About how glad I am that we met.'

He paused and by the time he began again she was surprised to see that a flush of embarrassment had darkened his cheeks.

'I'd never believed that I would ever find anyone who would mean as much to me as my career, but you mean more.'

At his stark admission Livvy's heart leapt again, but before she could comment on his intrinsically private revelations he was speaking again, his words hurried, as if he was trying to distract her from his unaccustomed candour.

'Not that I expect to get any more sleep once we *are* married,' he pointed out with a wicked gleam in his eyes. 'In fact, *sleeping* together will probably be the last thing we do, at least until we collapse with exhaustion.'

The distraction was complete.

'Daniel!' she exclaimed, her own cheeks burning as her imagination suddenly filled with erotic images of the two of them entwined on a bed, naked...

She shook her head to try to dispel such ideas until a more appropriate moment, glad that he couldn't read her mind.

She heard him draw in a sharp breath as she shook her head, then he dragged his eyes away to gaze fiercely at the table decoration of fragrant freesias for several long moments before he met her eyes again.

'I'm sorry, Livvy, that was very selfish of me,' he said quietly, his voice low and slightly uneven as he sought her gaze again. 'Would it spoil it for you if you couldn't have a big traditional wedding? I'd never really thought about it before, but I suppose that's what little girls grow up expecting.'

Livvy caught a fleeting glimpse of uncertainty in his eyes but it was swiftly hidden. She'd seen that expression several times in the last few weeks and had thought how incongruous it seemed in such a confident, self-reliant man.

It wasn't until she suddenly remembered one late-night conversation over tepid cups of coffee in the nurses' home that she began to understand the reason he wanted their marriage to be sooner rather than later.

They'd had an unusual case on the ward that day. An older woman, close to the upper end of her child-bearing years, had given birth to a baby she'd conceived for her daughter.

It had been an entirely do-it-yourself surrogacy arranged between the woman, her daughter and son-in-law, and Livvy's first reaction had been one of distaste.

It wasn't until she had spent some time in the delivery

room with the struggling older woman that she had heard about the daughter's earlier successful but very aggressive treatment for cancer which had left her unable to have any children of her own.

The joyous scene when the unusual family group had welcomed their baby into the world had affected Livvy deeply, especially when she learned that 'Grandad', whom the little boy was to be named for, had fought a losing battle with cancer, dying just weeks before the longed-for child was due.

Livvy had shed a few tears when she'd told Daniel about the family's background, marvelling that they'd found some way to create happiness out of so much tragedy.

Daniel had held her quietly, one arm around her shoulders as they'd monopolised one end of the settee in the dimly lit nurses' home lounge.

He'd been silent for a long time after she'd finished speaking, but she'd grown accustomed to that, happy to be with him without feeling the need to fill every second with meaningless chatter.

'I'll probably lose my mother first,' he murmured softly, and surprise robbed her of speech.

In spite of all the things they'd shared with each other in the days and weeks since they'd met, he'd said so little about his family that she'd begun to think he was all alone in the world.

'She's been confined to bed for years now, and just gets steadily worse,' he continued, threading his fingers between hers and bringing them up to his face to rest against his lips as if he wanted her help to stop any more painful words escaping.

'And your father?' she prompted softly, needing to hear the worst before she dared to offer sympathy.

'Inside, he's been dying by inches for years because he can't do anything for her. He feels so guilty because he's a doctor and the one person he most wants to be able to help is the one he can't…'

'How long has she been ill?'

'I can hardly remember a time when she was well. I can remember far enough back that my father was helping her to walk to the bathroom and then, eventually, having to carry her. Now he has to do everything—feed her, wash her, brush her hair.'

'But…doesn't he have any help, and…and what about his career?'

'He has some help, but he's cut his work down to part time so that he can be with her as much as possible. He says that the biggest tragedy is the fact that until fairly recently her mind stayed as sharp as ever but was trapped in a body that was bent on self-destruction.'

'He loves her,' Livvy said quietly, not having to make it a question.

Daniel gazed at her intently and she could see from his expression that she understood many of the things he hadn't voiced.

'Yes, he loves her,' Daniel said, pain making his voice even huskier than usual. 'And he tells her that he regrets the fact that they waited several years before they married when they could have spent that time together, and it's killing him that he knows he's going to lose her…'

Suddenly she understood the real reason behind his apparent headlong rush to get married. His own parents had enjoyed so few years of happy marriage before his mother's health had begun to deteriorate. As a consequence, he seemed to have developed a keener appreciation than most of how fleeting happiness could be.

Apparently, he'd coped with the idea of heartbreaking loss by keeping any possible entanglements at arm's length. Now, having decided to take the plunge, he didn't want to make the same mistake as his parents.

Livvy drew a swift breath for courage and offered her heart to him with her smile.

'Will you come shopping with me for my dress?' she asked softly. 'I'm off duty tomorrow afternoon.'

He gazed at her in silence for several seconds, his eyes probing hers deeply as if he needed to read the meaning behind her words in her soul.

Then he gave her an answering smile, the expression like the sun coming out after a long cold winter.

'Just tell me where and when,' he agreed, his hands capturing hers again in a fervent squeeze. 'If I have to get Mr den Haag to cover my shift for me in person I'll be there.'

So many of their colleagues were marrying at that time that it seemed as if they were always being invited to registry offices, churches or receptions.

'Our wedding was the best,' he growled huskily in her ear part way through the long weekend they'd managed to scrounge for a honeymoon.

They were submerged up to their necks in a gently bubbling Jacuzzi and Livvy wondered if she was ever going to be able to summon up the energy to move.

'Why?' she asked, replaying the events of their day and remembering the way it had been organised on a shoestring and all at breakneck speed.

In the last couple of months they'd been to some very

elaborate ceremonies and some very lavish parties to celebrate the marriages of some of their colleagues, while
theirs had been neither elaborate nor lavish.

'Simple. It was the best because this time I got to take
the bride to bed,' he declared wickedly as he swept her
up in his arms.

Totally ignoring her squeals of delighted surprise and
the torrents of water cascading across the floor, he carried her back to a circular bed as big as a helicopter
landing-pad and demonstrated the concept to their mu-
tual satisfaction.

A dragging ache in her hips and low down in her belly
drew Livvy back to the present, and she found Daniel
gazing at her with his straight brows drawn into a frown.
The vivid memories were still reverberating through her
head as she met his gaze.

He hadn't slept with the bride *this* time, she realised
with a fierce stab of something suspiciously like relief.
At least...not yet. There'd been no time between the
wedding and the accident.

A further thought tightened new bands of misery
around her heart. The fact that the two of them hadn't
had time to consummate their marriage could hardly
make a difference when the bride in question was already pregnant with their second child. He obviously
hadn't wanted to wait for their wedding night...

'Are you all right, Livvy?' he asked, drawing everyone's attention to her.

Hastily, she tried to compose her expression. Had her
thoughts been spread across her face for all to follow?
The sudden flush of heat in her cheeks told her she was
blushing hotly and she silently cursed.

Why was she still reacting like a teenager, for heaven's sake? She was a grown woman, due to be a mother in a couple of weeks, not some sixteen-year-old ninny. At least the turmoil had taken her mind off her aches and pains.

'I'm fine...really... Just enjoying getting my feet up and relaxing.'

If anything, his frown grew fiercer.

'You shouldn't be here in the first place,' he declared hotly. 'I don't know what your obstetrician was thinking of, giving you permission to go back to work this far into your pregnancy.'

Pat laughed, drawing the focus of his attention away from her, and she gave a silent sigh of relief.

'If I know Livvy, I don't think Duncan French had much to say about it,' she said with a wry chuckle. 'In fact, I think it's probably less wearing on Livvy, *and* the rest of us if she's kept busy. You wouldn't like to see what happens if we try to make her sit and twiddle her thumbs when there's work needs doing. Especially when we're in the sort of mess we are at the moment.'

'You don't need to tell me how stubborn the wretched woman can be,' he growled. 'There is a good reason why we're both called Jones.'

'You're *married*!' Cherry squeaked, breaking the startled silence and gazing from one to the other in amazement.

'Not any more,' Livvy tried to say, but her words were irretrievably lost under Daniel's deeper voice.

'Nearly three years ago,' he confirmed, 'so you can't tell me much about her that I don't already know.'

Livvy was still so surprised that he'd mentioned their now-defunct marriage that she hardly contributed to the flurry of questions and exclamations that followed the revelation. She was hardly able to concentrate on the answers he gave as she waited for him to mention their divorce and his recent remarriage...but he never did.

Was it out of deference to her heavily pregnant state that he left her colleagues thinking they were still married or was it simply because he was more preoccupied with her present state of health in a more immediate way?

He continued speaking politely enough but Livvy knew, from the way he kept glancing at her, that he was still far from happy with the situation.

There was an air of determination about him when their coffee break was over that told her that their threatened discussion wouldn't be long in coming.

'Could I have a word?' he said just as Livvy was waddling in Pat's wake to make her way out to the ward.

Drat, she thought, silently bemoaning the fact that she wasn't fast enough on her feet these days to get away from him.

She'd been hoping that they'd have had a positive result from the new Mrs Jones's ultrasound before he cornered her. Once he knew that their second child was safely on the way she reasoned that he'd be less likely to want to interfere in her plans for *her* baby.

'I know you said you were fine in front of your colleagues, but are you sure?' he asked quietly, with every evidence of concern. 'You haven't got much colour in your cheeks.'

The question was so unexpected that he completely took the wind out of her sails, and she sank back against the edge of the desk, suddenly needing the support.

She'd been ready to argue till her last breath if he

tried to tell her what to do or made any demands concerning the baby.

She'd begun to think that he'd never really cared for her—after all, it had been seven months since she'd last seen him and he'd made no attempt to see her in the interim. He hadn't even bothered to contact her to let her know that they were divorced.

Now, against all her expectations, his first concern was for *her*.

'I'm fine, really,' she murmured round the lump in her throat as sweeter memories assailed her.

This was the caring Daniel she remembered from the early days, and her heart ached anew for all they'd lost.

'If you need to rest you've only got to grab one of your colleagues,' he pointed out earnestly. 'It's obvious that they all care about you. Any one of them would be only too willing to do all the leg-work for you.'

'I know,' Livvy said with a smile. 'They're a smashing bunch. The trouble is, everything's so topsy-turvy at the moment that everyone's running just to stand still. Mostly, I'm spending my time going round talking to the patients to reassure them that everything's under control. I've also been acting as an unofficial liaison between the two wards because, with a mixed population, we're having to share resources.'

'And the delivery you did this morning?' One dark eyebrow rose to accentuate the pointed question.

'That wasn't work—that was the icing on the cake,' Livvy said with a beaming smile. 'She's an experienced mum who knew exactly what to expect, and everything happened so quickly and so smoothly that I was little more than a spectator.'

'Hmm. That's the first time I've heard *that* excuse for

a pregnant woman to do exactly what she wants whether she should or not!'

Livvy chuckled, marvelling how the atmosphere between the two of them could change so quickly.

She knew that he would never be reconciled to the fact that such a heavily pregnant woman was actually working to help others deliver their babies, and would probably be keeping a close eye on her, but at least he wasn't glaring at her any more. Perhaps now would be the time to have their discussion about—

'Sister!'

Cherry's voice preceded her and something in the tone alerted Livvy that their brief spell of calm was coming to an end.

Had she ever been that young and eager? Livvy found herself thinking as the fresh-faced young woman almost bounced with excitement at the door, her strictly non-regulation red and white pixie hat flopping from side to side.

'Yes, Cherry?' she said, subduing the grin that wanted to appear and turning it into a patient smile.

'It's Mrs Owens, Sister. We've been timing her contractions and I think you ought to check her. They're getting very close together.'

'Thank you, Nurse,' said Daniel, as he held out both hands towards Livvy to pull her to her feet. 'We'll be there as soon as we can.'

'We?' Livvy panted indignantly as she straightened her smock and tried to ignore the warmth in her tingling hands where he'd grasped them. 'You don't need to wait for me. I can get there under my own steam.'

'All right. Have it your own way,' he said, with both hands held up in submission as he turned to walk away.

Livvy couldn't help the chuckle that escaped her when she heard him muttering on his way out, knowing he was doing it deliberately just loud enough for her to hear a litany that started with 'independent' and progressed through 'stubborn' and 'pig-headed' before he was out of hearing range.

She was still smiling when she joined him beside Nerys Owens's bed, just in time to see him work his familiar magic on the apprehensive young woman.

'Everything's going beautifully,' he told her reassuringly. 'In fact, I think you're just about ready to transfer to the luxury accommodations along the corridor. Christmas carols and decorations will be thrown in free.'

The young woman frowned briefly before her face cleared.

'Oh, you mean the delivery room!' she exclaimed, and flicked a glance towards her equally young-looking husband. 'Is it really time?'

Livvy saw what Cherry had meant when she'd said some of the fathers-to-be in the ward had turned green during Megan Williams's delivery.

'Mr Owens might need to be re-christened Kermit before the morning's over,' she warned quietly as Daniel joined her at the end of the bed.

She saw the assessing gaze he trained on the young man's colour and the nod that told her he'd understood what she'd meant. Her gaze lingered for a moment on his profile and she visually traced the slight bump on the lean perfection of his aristocratic nose.

She couldn't help remembering the day he'd received that bump and the fact that he'd blamed it on her.

It had only been a couple of days after their first meeting when she'd heard from one of the other nurses that he was a member of the hospital's rugby team—well, he was partly Welsh *and* a doctor so it had been almost expected of him.

Never having dated much, she'd never developed an interest in the game—hadn't even realised that the hospital fielded a team.

Having heard that he was playing, that afternoon had found her making her way towards the cheers and jeers of the supporters as St Augustine's had taken on a team from one of the London hospitals.

One minute the game had been in full flow, with two sets of mud-caked men charging towards her end of the pitch flinging the oval ball apparently indiscriminately from one to the other. The next minute there had been an almighty crash and a tangle of arms and legs as the figure at the head of the pack had been brought down.

It hadn't been until the unknown nurse beside her had exclaimed aloud that Livvy had realised that Daniel had been the man at the bottom of the pile of heaving bodies, and it hadn't been until later that evening when he'd been nursing his broken nose that he'd blamed her presence for distracting him and causing the disaster.

'Right, Mr Owens,' Daniel said briskly, snapping Livvy's attention away from its preoccupation with his profile. 'If you'd like to come with me a minute, we'll let the nurses get your wife organised.'

Livvy spared the two of them a glance as Daniel led the terrified father-to-be away, and she couldn't help comparing Mr Owens's slight, almost boyish frame with Daniel's far more imposing height and breadth.

'Where is he taking John? He will bring him back in time for the baby to be born?' Nerys demanded with renewed panic in her voice.

'Don't worry, he's taking him along to the delivery room to put a gown on. He'll look like one of the television doctors by the time we get there,' Livvy joked as she set her patient's mind at rest.

Her own mind was a different matter.

It had taken Nerys Owens's question to make her realise that she and Daniel had automatically slipped into their seamless routine of working together, with hardly a word needed for each to know what the other meant.

How many times in the past had he drawn a nervous father aside for a surreptitious pep-talk? All she knew was that those he spoke to usually sailed through their wives' deliveries, if not enthusiastically then at least supportively, adding to the special atmosphere surrounding the miracle of birth.

She didn't doubt for a minute that he would work the same magic on John Owens and that in a few days the Owens family would leave the hospital, wondering what on earth they had ever worried about.

In the meantime, she needed to organise Nerys Owens's speedy transfer to the delivery suite just as soon as she made certain that Jill Simpson had been safely removed to her bed on the ward upstairs.

It was in the middle of this organisation that Dewi finally arrived with her trolley full of equipment to run the ultrasound test on the new Mrs Jones.

# CHAPTER FIVE

LIVVY was pulled two ways.

Of course she wanted to be there for the ultrasound and wanted it to show that the baby was fine.

That would mean that she could look forward to Daniel taking Alice away so that she wouldn't have the woman's presence on the ward as a reminder of everything that had gone wrong in her life.

Unfortunately, it would also mean that Daniel wouldn't be there any more, and that was something she didn't want to think about.

At least when they were busy it was just like when they had worked together at St Augustine's before her world had fallen apart. If she concentrated on the minute-to-minute events of their time together she could almost forget the dreadful seven months in between, as if they had been nothing more than a shadowy nightmare.

Livvy gave herself a mental shake and set about organising Nerys Owens's transfer along the corridor before she joined Dewi and Alice Jones behind the curtains drawn around her bed. Silently, she made herself a promise that as soon as the test was over, and Alice Jones had been settled down, she would hurry along to see if she could be there for Nerys Owens's baby to arrive.

That always supposed that the ultrasound gave good news. If not, she might find herself in the uneasy position of having to offer comfort and consolation to the one person in the world to whom she didn't want to speak.

'I am so sorry you have been kept waiting so long,' Dewi was saying as she began to unravel the electrical connections from several strands of multicoloured tinsel and prepared to set everything up. 'It must be so uncomfortable, having to wait so long.'

Livvy had to hide a grimace of her own when she thought about how long it had been since she'd sent the two cups of tea to this patient. She would have had difficulty waiting five minutes after drinking that much, let alone...

'After I was told to go to the pregnant lady I was called back down to Casualty to scan a patient with the kidney stones so I have come back to you as swiftly as it is possible.'

Alice Jones lay quietly as the torrent of words poured over her, her face white with tension as she gazed intently at the screen when the first indistinct images appeared, and Livvy couldn't help feeling sympathetic.

No matter what the woman had done, Livvy couldn't wish the baby any harm, especially as it would be so closely related to her own child.

'Ah, now, look at this,' Dewi said, as she drew the probe smoothly over the well-oiled skin and the image on the monitor grew more distinct. 'I am seeing where your little one is situated inside you and if you will be so good as to look just here...' she reached out to point at the screen with one slender finger '...you will see the rhythmic pulses of your baby's heart.'

'The heart is still beating?' quavered the poor woman lying flat on the bed. 'My baby's still alive?'

Livvy had to bite her lip to control its quiver when

she heard in her voice just how much Alice Jones wanted her baby to live.

As she lay there, helpless, bruised and obviously afraid, Alice looked every one of her years. Nearly ten years younger, Livvy was consumed with jealousy when she wondered just what Daniel had seen in the woman that he had so easily abandoned his wife for her.

Was it the fact that Alice had borne him a son when he and Livvy hadn't intended starting their family yet? Had he felt morally bound to give her and her child the support of his name? If he'd known that Livvy, too, was carrying his child, would he have stayed with her?

'Yes, your baby is still very much still alive,' Dewi assured her as she programmed the machine to make a copy of the scan. 'If you will like, I will give you the picture so you can look at it and one day you will like to show to baby when it is big.'

'Oh, thank you so much. I would like a picture, then I can show it to the baby's father.'

Livvy saw her peering at the technician's name-tag with a slight frown.

'Your name is so unusual,' Alice said, relief obviously making her relaxed enough to make conversation. 'What part of the world did your family come from?'

'We come originally from Thailand where my father was with the diplomatic corps. When he had the posting to come to England he is bringing his family with him and I am staying here to learn about Western medicine before I go back to do the same thing in the big new hospital near to our home.'

'And how do you pronounce your name? What is the correct Thai way?'

'Davey,' Dewi said with a giggle. 'It makes me sound like a boy in your country.'

'Oh, but what a coincidence!' the older woman exclaimed. 'That is the name I gave my son!'

Livvy didn't know how she'd got out of the cubicle. Had she just rudely barged her way out through the curtains without a word or had she actually managed to make her excuses before she'd hurried across the ward and into the nearest staff toilet?

'Davey,' she whispered when she'd shut herself in a cubicle and leant weakly back against the door. 'She called their son Davey...'

The only person she'd ever discussed baby names with had been Daniel, and they'd laughingly decided that in honour of his father their hypothetical son would one day be called David.

'How *could* he,' she moaned in anguish, the tears starting to trickle down her cheeks. It had been one of the few consolations left to her that, whichever sex their child turned out to be, she would be able to give it the name Daniel had helped her to choose.

How could she do that now when he'd given that name to his other child first?

The trickle of tears became a torrent as she remembered that dreadful day seven months ago, the day which had been the beginning of the end of her happy marriage.

It had been no more and no less hectic than any other day in St Augustine's busy Maternity department until Miss Webster had been brought in.

She had been full term and already in strong labour when she'd arrived, and as Livvy's previous patient had just delivered a healthy daughter and been settled into the ward she'd been free to attend to the unexpected intake.

It had appeared that, although she'd been resident in the area, Alice hadn't been attending the antenatal department at the hospital so she hadn't met any of the midwives.

Having settled her into bed, Livvy had sat down with her to ask the questions that would form the basis of her case notes.

There hadn't been enough time to build up any sort of bond of trust between them before suddenly the woman had gone into transition and had rapidly entered the second stage of labour.

'Where's Daniel?' the woman demanded in a panic-stricken voice as she resisted all Livvy's efforts to calm her down and get her to concentrate on her breathing. 'He said he'd be here when I needed him. Where is he?'

'Did you let him know you were in labour?' Livvy prompted, wondering who the elusive Daniel was. Miss Webster definitely wasn't married, according to her hastily taken details, so perhaps he was the baby's father? Or perhaps a supportive friend?

'He works here,' she said shortly as she panted for breath between contractions which seemed to be almost continuous now. 'He's Daniel Jones...the gynaecologist and obstetrician. Please...will you call him? Quickly. Tell him I need him...'

Livvy was too surprised to do anything else, her hand reaching out automatically for the phone to arrange for the switchboard to page him.

So far there had been nothing in the progress of her patient's labour that made Livvy think that they were going to need Daniel's help. But perhaps her patient knew something she hadn't told her, and if it helped her to calm down it was worth the call.

Even so, it was nearly half an hour before Daniel arrived, the Caesarean he was performing in Theatre necessarily taking precedence over Miss Webster's needs.

When Daniel finally entered the room his eyes had gone to Livvy first to find out what the problem was, but as soon as he began to speak her patient recognised him.

'Daniel… You came,' she said, and burst into tears.

Livvy felt almost invisible as she continued to manage the older woman's labour while her husband focused entirely on talking to their patient to calm her down.

He chidingly bullied her into concentrating on what her body was trying to do and gently encouraged her to push just one more time.

When the little boy was safely delivered and Livvy wrapped him up to hand him to his mother for the first time, it was to Daniel that the proud new mother held up the little scrap for inspection, for all the world as if he were the father.

'Look, Daniel,' Miss Webster crowed as she unwrapped the tiny mite just far enough to examine his fingers and toes. 'He's even got the Jones toes.'

Livvy froze in the act of writing her notes and turned in disbelief to gaze at the tiny feet.

As if in slow motion, she watched Daniel lean forward to look and saw him smile his slightly lopsided smile— the one that always made her breath catch in her throat and her heart skip a beat with anticipation when directed at her.

This time it chilled her to the marrow.

'They're just like yours, aren't they?' Alice Webster

crooned as she stroked the strangely curled little digits with a gentle finger. 'You said they were inherited from your father's side of the family and now they've been passed on to my baby.'

Livvy could barely remember the rest of that shift. It was lucky that Alice Webster had been the last of her patients because she must have moved through her remaining duties like an automaton.

The thing she could recall with nightmare clarity was the terrible argument that had exploded between Daniel and herself when they'd reached the flat that evening.

It hadn't seemed to matter what she'd said or how often she'd asked—he had utterly refused to tell her anything about Alice Webster's place in his life.

The argument had raged intermittently for several hours, but when she'd seen that adamant look come into his eyes she'd finally realised that he wasn't going to change his mind.

'I gave her my promise,' he repeated stubbornly, as if that was the last word on the subject.

That only incensed Livvy even more.

'You made some promises to me, too,' she pointed out, feeling the ominous prickle behind her eyes and silently cursing her recently discovered pregnancy for messing with her emotional control.

What disastrous timing. How could she share her momentous news with him when there was so much ugliness between them?

'Do your promises to her take precedence over the ones you made me?' she demanded, blinking furiously so that not a single tear should fall.

'I promised to love, honour and cherish you,' he said

in a voice grown even huskier after a night without sleep and a day full of arguments.

'And *do* you?' she challenged bluntly. 'How can you honour me when there's a child in St Augustine's that shares a remarkable resemblance to you, even down to an inherited deformity?'

As ever, he set his mouth in a stubborn line, asking only that she trust him.

She had no option but to share their bed that night, going to sleep as far away from him as she could manage with her back firmly turned towards him.

She woke up the next morning to find Daniel's arms wrapped around her, her head pillowed on his shoulder, the way it had been right from the first night of their marriage.

For a moment Livvy smiled as she savoured the happy intimacy and shifted the position of her head slightly so that she could look at her sleeping husband.

'Don't go yet,' Daniel murmured sleepily, his voice a sexy growl as he tightened his arms around her and rubbed his beard-roughened cheek over the top of her head. 'I missed this last night.'

Those few words were enough for her to remember the black cloud hanging over her happiness and she rolled swiftly across the bed.

It might have been the sudden movement or the gut-wrenching disappointment when she remembered his adamant refusal to tell her what was going on but, whatever was the cause, she suddenly had to run to the bathroom to endure her first racking bout of morning sickness.

It was the last straw.

\*  \*  \*

From a distance of seven months, Livvy looked back at her last-ditch demand that he talked to her and his continued refusal, then her hasty search for another job and somewhere to live before her own pregnancy became obvious.

When even those drastic methods hadn't changed his mind her heart had finally shattered and she'd contacted the first firm of solicitors she'd come to for advice about divorce.

She'd only been back once, for Sarah Jones's funeral just weeks after their separation.

During the journey, she decided to make certain that she spent her time close to her father-in-law. She'd been worried that Daniel might try to corner her and she couldn't have borne it if he compounded his father's unhappiness, by creating a scene.

As it was, she needn't have worried.

'Livvy. Thank you for coming.' Daniel greeted her at the church, sparing her no more than a brief nod before he welcomed the next group of mourners behind her.

It was the same at the house.

'May I take your coat?' he asked when she entered the spacious hallway, his voice no warmer than if they were strangers, then he directed her into the lounge as if she'd never been in the house before.

To give him the benefit of the doubt, it didn't look as if he'd slept properly for weeks, his eyes dull and darkly shadowed and his face quite grey with exhaustion.

She paused in the doorway to look back at him, and just for a crazy moment she was swamped by compassion. He looked so...so lost and alone, and all she could think of doing was wrapping her arms around him to offer comfort.

For just a moment she wondered if she'd made a terrible mistake in leaving Daniel. She still loved him as much as ever, and although there was yet little outward evidence, she was now carrying his child while he seemed far from happy.

What if she'd jumped to conclusions and there was a perfectly rational explanation for everything that had happened?

Once again her mind was buzzing with possibilities.

Had that woman, Alice Webster, been some unacknowledged relative of Daniel's father that her child had inherited the same curled toes that she'd teased Daniel about?

Was she, perhaps, an illegitimate daughter whose presence had to be hidden while Sarah Jones was alive?

Perhaps, now that circumstances had forced them to meet, they should pause in their headlong rush to destroy the last bonds between them. Perhaps she should take this opportunity to sit down with him and talk everything over. Perhaps, now, he would be ready to tell her the reason for all the hurtful secrecy.

At that moment, the front door opened again to admit another mourner. Indecisive, Livvy hovered for a moment, waiting for Daniel to direct her through to the other room, but as soon as he helped the newcomer off with her coat she turned into his arms and rested her head on his shoulder.

With a gasp of shock she recognised Alice Webster.

Without a second thought she whirled and made her way to her father-in-law's side and there she remained, steadfastly ignoring the fact that Daniel stayed out in the hallway with the woman.

\*    \*    \*

In some ways, those events seemed to have happened to a different person in another lifetime, but just at the moment it felt as if the wounds were fresh and raw.

Was her life going to be one long round of meetings with Daniel in which she got to see him just long enough to remember everything she was missing before Alice Webster stole him away again?

She hiccuped twice in quick succession and scowled at the resulting kick the baby gave her.

'There's nothing like a swift reminder of the facts of life,' she muttered as she blew her nose and emerged from the toilet stall to soak a paper towel with water and hold it to her burning eyes.

What had she been thinking about?

*This* time would be the last her path would be crossing Daniel's. Now that she knew he'd married Alice and their union was to be blessed with a second child she would have to forget all those hopeless little fantasies about her handsome husband coming to find her and swearing he'd loved her all along. It just wasn't going to happen.

She drew in as deep a breath as the restrictions on her ribs would allow and glared at her reflection in the mirror over the basin, deliberately ignoring the smiling Santa someone had stuck in each corner.

Her eyes were red, her nose was shiny and her silvery blonde hair was starting to straggle untidily around her face like a limp dishmop.

'Tell me, madam, how does it feel to be Mrs Goodyear Blimp?' she asked, then pulled a face as she tried to lean a little closer while she fiddled with her hair to neaten it.

Thank goodness there were only two weeks left to her

due date. She didn't know if she could put up with much more of this.

Suddenly the girdle of muscles around her uterus tightened and she had to grip the edge of the basin while she concentrated on her breathing, waiting for the pain to die away.

She'd been experiencing Braxton Hicks contractions for some weeks now but that was the heftiest one yet. All she hoped was that all the practising her body was doing would lead to a comparatively quick and easy birth when the time came.

'Speaking about when the time comes,' she muttered, hearing footsteps hurrying past the door as she straightened her shoulders and gave her back a rub, 'I should be out there, seeing what I can do to help. That'll keep my mind off my own problems.'

It was only a small pep-talk, but if she was lucky it would work just as well as Daniel's did on the expectant fathers. They went in the delivery room as trembling mice and came out as confident fathers. Quite a transformation…

Her own was less obvious, but would have to do. The trick was to let people see what they wanted to see, and in her case that was a pregnant nurse in control of herself and her destiny with plenty of time and energy left over to help others along the way.

'And it's all done with mirrors,' she whispered as she made her way towards the delivery room. At least she could console herself that she was going to be the one to give Daniel the good news about the baby.

'Livvy?' Pat called before she'd gone more than a dozen paces.

She sighed, suddenly feeling more than a little weary.

'More problems?' she asked when she saw the sheets of paper Pat was brandishing.

'Luckily, not this time.' She turned the top sheet so that Livvy could read it. 'The notes from Mrs Simpson's own antenatal hospital finally arrived.'

'Do I say better late than never?' Livvy asked wryly. 'Is there anything there we need to know about for her post-operative care?'

'As far as I can see, everything was perfectly straight-forward until the twins got themselves into the wrong position,' Pat offered. 'Certainly nothing major.'

'I'll take these and show them to Daniel before I put them with our notes,' Livvy said, and set off again to-wards the delivery suite.

With a swift detour to don gown and gloves, she re-versed through the swing doors to enter the room, and in spite of her determination her heart stammered in her throat when the first thing she heard was Daniel's voice.

'You're doing beautifully, Nerys,' he said with a world of encouragement in his tone. 'John and I can see the baby's head now.'

'And it doesn't take after your grandfather,' quipped the young man, proving conclusively to Livvy that Daniel's man-to-man words of wisdom had worked their miracle again. 'Girl or boy, it's got a lovely head of hair.'

'Good. You'll have something to grab hold of to pull it out, then,' grumbled the young woman, her freckles more obvious than ever under the clinically bright light. 'I don't want to do this any longer.'

Daniel must have caught sight of Livvy out of the corner of his eye because suddenly he was looking straight at her with a wicked twinkle in his eyes above the top of his mask.

'Sister, if you'd managed to push your baby that far out, would you want to stop now?' he demanded.

'I'd certainly find it difficult to walk around or sit down,' she retorted with a wink for the exhausted young woman. 'Especially when the baby's head is so close to coming.'

'Is it really close?' Nerys pleaded tearfully, turning automatically to the other woman in the room for reassurance. 'It feels as if I've been doing this for hours and getting nowhere.'

'Do you want to see?' Livvy offered, and took the couple of steps necessary to locate a mirror left in the room for that specific purpose. 'If John can support your shoulders for a minute...'

She held the mirror between the young mother's spread knees and tilted it in approximately the right direction.

'Can you see now?'

'Tilt a bit more, please. Oh!' The exclamation emerged on a soft breath as she caught her first sight of her baby, the dark head of hair already visible as the head crowned. 'It's nearly here,' she whispered with reverence in her voice as she looked up at her equally young husband. 'The baby's nearly here...look.'

There wasn't time for any more conversation as the next contraction began to take hold of her and Livvy put the mirror aside again to take up her position on the other side of Daniel.

This time Nerys pushed with a will, barely stopping to draw in another breath as she strained to push her baby into the world.

Each time a contraction faded she asked one of them for a progress report until it was easier for Livvy to keep the mirror to hand.

It wasn't long before there was the sharp sound of a baby's cry in the room and Daniel was presenting the couple with their son to the soft strains of 'Unto us is born a son' in the corridor.

'Oh, he's so beautiful,' Nerys sobbed happily as she cradled her noisy infant. 'Absolutely perfect.'

'And with a perfect set of lungs,' Daniel murmured in an aside to Livvy, making her chuckle.

Their laughter was interrupted when Amy Aldarini stuck her head around the door and gave the two of them a sharply speculative look.

'Have you lot nearly finished in here? I've got another one coming to the boil upstairs.'

'Hello, Livvy,' Amy said.

Knowing the efficiency of the hospital grapevine, Livvy was suddenly aware of the significance of the thoughtful expression in her colleague's eyes and was forced to make introductions. 'Amy Aldarini, Midwife, this is Dr Daniel Jones, Obs and Gynae. We shouldn't be more than a quarter of an hour or so. Will that do?'

'Should do fine unless Mum had dynamite with her breakfast,' Amy quipped with a grin. 'Catch up with you later...' She disappeared again.

'Speaking of breakfast,' Daniel murmured beside her, 'is there any chance that I could grab some food? We never got to the wedding reception and I'm starving.'

After the light-hearted banter of the last three-quarters of an hour his words were like a shower of icy water.

To cover her sudden shock Livvy made a show of consulting the watch pinned to the front of her smock, but it took several seconds before she could focus on the numbers.

How could she have let herself forget that the two of them were no longer married colleagues, working at the same hospital with an enviable record for delivering healthy babies to happy parents?

Daniel was no longer her loving husband but, as of this morning, now belonged to Alice, the new Mrs Jones.

'If you like, you could go now,' she said coolly, glancing in his direction without actually looking at him. 'I could finish up in here. Oh, by the way, the technician finally made it up to the ward to do the ultrasound. It doesn't look as if the baby has suffered any ill-effects from the crash.'

There was a strange silence in the room and she could almost feel him frowning at her changed attitude, but she resisted the temptation to look at his expression as she turned away to gather up the used instruments.

'Livvy?'

There was an air of strain in his husky voice but she couldn't let it affect her.

'Yes?' she replied with all the nonchalance she could muster.

He paused, obviously expecting her to turn and face him but she steeled herself not to.

He'd always been far too perceptive where she was concerned, and there was no way she was going to let him know that his defection could still hurt her this way. Nor did she want to reveal that having to pass on news about his new wife and baby was like having to drive a dagger through her own heart. She'd never felt such jealousy before, and wasn't proud of it now.

The more time she spent with him and the more often

she feasted her eyes on him the harder it was going to be to shut him out of her mind when the snow cleared and he was able to take Alice away. It was better—for the sake of her sanity, if nothing else—if she started to push him away now.

'I just wanted to say thank you,' he said quietly, his voice telling her he was far too close for comfort, 'for letting me know about Alice and the baby. Now all I have to do is find out whether my father's out of Theatre so I can let him know.'

# CHAPTER SIX

DANIEL followed the directions and found himself outside the doors of the surgical ward.

Until he'd actually rung through to find out how his father was faring under the orthopaedic surgeon's knife he hadn't realised how many hours had passed since the accident.

His first inclination when they'd all arrived at the hospital had been to stay near to his father until he knew how the operation had gone.

His father's injuries had looked horrific, even to someone who saw the gorier side of life on a daily basis, and the fact that it was his father's bone Daniel saw sticking out through lacerated flesh made it worse than ever.

By the time they'd been transported to hospital logic had kicked in and Daniel was able to admit that, now they were running fluids into him to replace the oceans of blood he seemed to be losing, his father's injuries weren't actually life-threatening.

Logic also told Daniel that because Alice had remained conscious throughout the horrors of the crash and their slow extraction from the shattered vehicle her need for support and patient understanding was actually the greater.

Poor Alice.

This certainly wasn't the wedding day she'd hoped for. First, the unexpected weather front, dumping inches of snow, and then the disaster of the accident.

It was bad enough that his father might be incapacitated for months while his hip mended, and would require a great deal of patient handling if he wasn't to explode with frustration at being confined. That was going to cause a great deal of stress all round.

Then there was the possibility that Alice might lose the baby.

No wonder she had wanted to cling so closely, barely letting him out of her sight. The fact that little Davey had escaped the crash virtually unscathed, and was now more or less happily settled in the children's ward for observation, had been the only piece of good news Daniel had been able to give her.

It had been almost a relief that he'd had the excuse of staff shortages in the department to allow him to occupy his hands and brain, otherwise he would have been close to cracking too. It wasn't as if he could actually do anything to help her, in spite of the fact that this was his speciality.

He relived the moment when he'd looked up from pushing Alice in the wheelchair to find Livvy, standing in front of him.

He'd nearly lost it then.

He'd known that she was working at Bryn Madoc Memorial and had thought that he was prepared to see her but all his mental lectures about staying calm and civil if he bumped into her had vaporised in an instant.

'Bloody woman,' he muttered forcefully, quite startling a passing orderly who gave him a wide berth on his way into the department.

Why hadn't she contacted him to let him know she was pregnant? Not only did he have the *right* to know that he was going to be a father but she should have known that he would *want* to know.

His heart clenched with the knowledge of all the weeks and months he had missed of his child's development. He didn't know the simplest things.

How long had it been before she'd realised she was pregnant? Had she been very sick? How many weeks had it been before she'd felt the first faint fluttering movements deep inside? Did she know what sex the baby was? Had she decided what names she was going to use?

He felt the frown pleat his forehead when he remembered the names they'd joked about using for their hypothetical children, and his quiet dismay when Alice had chosen the same name for her son. Had Livvy been disappointed too? Did she even know?

God, it had been an awful seven months since she'd left. Everything that could have gone wrong seemed to have done so.

First it had been his mother's death and the inevitable emotional, practical and legal aftermath. It had hardly been surprising that his father had relied so heavily on him during those initial weeks as a mixture of guilt and relief had warred for supremacy.

He'd longed for the comfort and security of having Livvy waiting for him when he got home, the only person he'd ever felt comfortable about confiding in.

Unfortunately, apart from her fleeting presence at his mother's funeral, when he'd been barely holding himself and his father together, she seemed to have disappeared off the face of the earth, and Daniel honestly hadn't had a minute free to find her.

At first sight, tracing her hadn't struck him as a dif-

ficult task because he'd believed that she'd stayed somewhere in the vicinity of St Augustine's.

When he'd realised that she'd resigned her post he'd
widened the area of his search to other maternity wards,
gradually going further and further afield.

Daniel's pride had hurt that he'd had to ask around,
but once he'd discovered that apparently none of her
former colleagues at St Augustine's had a forwarding
address he became really concerned.

It had been a chance comment of his father's when
Daniel had asked him about his conversation with Livvy
after the funeral which had prompted him to search the
other side of the country.

Daniel had just tracked Livvy down to Bryn Madoc
Memorial and had been making plans to confront her
when Alice had surfaced in his life again and everything
had been thrown into turmoil once more.

'Excuse me, sir. Are you waiting for someone or are
you lost?'

The security guard's polite enquiry suddenly made
him realise how long he'd been standing outside the
ward. No wonder the poor man thought he was behaving
suspiciously.

'I've been gathering the courage to visit my father,'
he said, stretching the truth more than somewhat. 'He's
just come out of surgery after a car crash this morning.'

'Ah, well, it's understandable that you're a bit nervous
about it if you're not used to being in hospitals,' the
guard said kindly. 'If you go straight through the doors
you're bound to see one of the ward staff and they'll
take you to see him if he's allowed visitors yet. I hope
he's doing all right.'

Daniel didn't correct the man's misapprehension. The

thought of what he would say if he knew he'd been talking to a doctor was the one thing that lightened his mood.

He was aware that the smartly uniformed man stood and watched him through the tinsel-framed safety-glass panels in the door until he reached the door of the ward sister's office and stuck his head in.

'Probably thinks I'll chicken out,' Daniel muttered under his breath before he knocked on the open door to attract her attention.

It only took a moment to tell her who he was looking for and confirm that he'd come to the right place.

A brief mention of his professional qualifications gained him a host of details about the success of his father's operation and its favourable prognosis, and was the open sesame to an immediate visit.

'Daniel,' his father croaked as soon as he appeared by the bedside, his eyes popping open almost as soon as his son reached him.

'I should have known you'd be too stubborn to stay asleep when they want you to,' Daniel teased gently, and pulled up a chair beside the bed.

'Any news?' his father prompted, his free hand reaching across to grasp Daniel's fiercely.

Daniel returned the pressure and gazed down at their clasped hands. Until that moment, he hadn't really noticed just how much alike their hands were and that thought prompted a critical examination of the man lying helpless in the bed in front of him.

His father certainly wasn't looking his best so soon after a major reconstructive operation, but he was still a very good-looking man. If Daniel wore half as well he would be able to count himself lucky, especially if his life was filled with the sort of anguish his father had been forced to endure year after year.

'Daniel, for God's sake,' his father broke in, his face deathly pale and sounding quite frantic, 'tell me what's happened?'

'Sorry, Dad,' he apologised, suddenly realising that the staff probably hadn't had the chance to tell him how things had gone. 'They think the operation was a complete success. They've managed to plate and screw you back together and within just a few weeks you'll be able to—'

'Not *me*,' his father interrupted, dragging his hand away to flap it dismissively. 'What about Alice and the baby? And Davey? What's happened to them? Oh, son, I feel so guilty. If only you had been driving.'

'Hey, Dad, calm down.' Daniel grabbed for his father's hand again and squeezed it tightly between his own. 'It probably would have happened anyway, given the road conditions. Alice is fine—they all are.'

'You're sure? Absolutely sure?' he demanded.

'Absolutely,' Daniel repeated. 'She's had the ultrasound and all is well. The heart is beating strongly. And Davey's got the nurses wrapped round his little finger already. The children's ward will never be the same.'

'Thank God,' his father breathed, and as he finally relaxed back onto the pillows the colour began to seep into his cheeks. 'I was so afraid I'd killed them.'

Daniel spent a few minutes reassuring his father that all was well, but his concentration was divided. He was talking about Davey and Alice and the growing hope that the baby she carried was unaffected by the crash, but all the while he had an urgent need to bring the conversation round to Livvy.

Finally he saw an opening and took it.

'The sister who organised the scan was Livvy,' he said, barely aware in his preoccupation that he was being so blunt until he saw his father's eyes narrow with speculation.

'You mean we ended up in the same hospital?' he asked with a rusty chuckle. 'Well, at least it saved you a journey. You mentioned that you were thinking of paying her a visit after the wedding.'

'Did you know she's pregnant?' Daniel demanded, this time remembering just in time to keep his voice down out of deference to his surroundings and his father's temporarily fragile state of health, but his soft voice was definitely at odds with the way he was feeling.

Livvy had obviously let slip enough details during their conversation after the funeral for his father to be able to direct his search towards Wales. If she'd also told him about the baby and his father had kept the information to himself...

'Pregnant?' the older man exclaimed, clearly shocked. 'Good God!'

'It looks as if she's nearly full term, but due to a flu epidemic causing shortages of staff, and that bloody snow, she's actually still working.'

His father was silent for long moments, lying with his eyes closed, and Daniel felt his frustration growing when he realised that the poor man was in no fit state to be badgered. Now that his mind had been set at rest about Davey, Alice and the baby, he probably wanted nothing more than to sleep off the rest of his anaesthetic.

'You're as protective as ever,' his father growled softly as he opened his eyes the merest crack. 'You're obviously still smitten so what are you going to do about it?'

Daniel didn't bother to contradict him. He knew it wouldn't do him any good. The wretched man was far too perceptive, even when he was doped up to the eyeballs on analgesics.

'I don't know *what* I'm going to do yet, but one thing is certain—no child of mine is going to grow up without knowing its father.'

As soon as Livvy arrived back on the ward she noticed the air of suppressed excitement building while the other patients waited for Nerys and her new baby to return.

'Having several babies arrive so quickly is making them all very hopeful,' she commented wryly as she supervised the distribution of the meals around the ward.

'You mean, the rest of them are hoping they're going to cough and, hey presto, there's a baby!' Pat Lersh said with a laugh.

'If only it *was* that easy!' Livvy groaned. 'The more I think about it the more I feel like asking for an epidural or even a Caesarean!'

'Chicken!' Pat taunted. 'You're one of the professionals. You can't afford to let the side down. Anyway, you're luckier than most. Your husband is in the trade, too, so you'll get preferential treatment.'

'Ha!' Livvy snorted inelegantly.

She swiftly suppressed the stab of discomfort at the reminder that Pat believed she and Daniel were still married. She was going to have to explain all that misunderstanding at some stage, but wasn't in any hurry to do it now. There were too many ears about and the whole thing could end up being very embarrassing, especially with her replacement lying in the bed on the other side of the room.

'You're joking, of course,' she grumbled in answer to Pat's teasing. 'If there are several of us in labour at once you know darn well that the professional will be left to get on with it because she knows what's happening, whereas the poor "amateur" needs all the help she can get!'

'You could be right,' Pat conceded with a laugh. 'You'll just have to time it right.'

'Talking about timing,' Livvy said, determined to change the direction of the conversation, 'has there been any sort of update on the various Christmassy events for the people stuck here over the holiday? I know there's supposed to be a carol concert this evening and Christmas dinner tomorrow midday, but what about Father Christmas visiting the wards?'

'As far as I know, the choir—in its much depleted form—will be paying a brief visit to each ward some time during the evening. There was a message a little while ago, asking for volunteer voices to swell the ranks, so if you've got any sort of a voice…?'

Pat left the question hanging tantalisingly in the air and Livvy pulled a face. Her participation would depend on how busy the ward was this evening so it was better if she didn't make any promises. Anyway, she could use the fact that she wasn't *officially* staff at the moment as a get-out clause.

It wasn't that her voice was bad—in fact, it was a lot better than most—but in an area of Britain noted for superlative singing she was hesitant to put herself forward.

Now if it had been Daniel they'd been asking, that

was another matter. He might be only half-Welsh, but he seemed to have inherited all of the genes for musical ability with a beautiful rich tenor voice.

Her thoughts switched instantly to the first time she'd heard him, the day they'd decided to start decorating the living room of the flat.

She'd honestly thought he'd put a CD on to listen to while he worked, and had wondered whose voice it was, sending shivers up her spine—until she'd walked in the room with a reviving tray of coffee and had realised the voice had been his.

Once, she'd made the mistake of letting him know the effect it had on her. After that, he'd often teased her, by singing brief snatches of romantic arias as a prelude to snatching her up in his arms and rushing her, shrieking and laughing, to the bedroom.

'As for Christmas meals,' Pat continued, dragging Livvy's attention back to her immediate surroundings, 'you'll see in a few minutes that we usually have something festive with the evening meal, such as mince pies, but, regardless of snow and flu epidemics, there'll be Christmas dinner with all the trimmings tomorrow at midday just after Father Christmas does his rounds.'

'Pretty much the same whichever hospital you're in,' Livvy commented, hoping the flush her heated imaginings had brought to her cheeks could be attributed to anything but their real cause.

'Under more normal circumstances,' Pat continued, apparently oblivious to Livvy's heightened colour, 'on our ward it usually means that the younger relatives can be here for the handing out of gifts and then can go home for their own lunches. That leaves the possibility of another quieter visit later in the day for the adults.'

'But with all that snow out there, who knows what's going to happen?' Livvy pointed out. 'Some visitors might not dare make the journey.'

'And others might get stuck here,' Pat added darkly.

'Well, it's obviously a matter of wait and see while we get on with the routine stuff,' Livvy concluded as she tried to make herself comfortable enough to sit down to eat. As a patient, her meal was being delivered to the ward, but she'd opted to eat it in Sister's office to keep Pat company.

It felt quite strange to be caught halfway between being a member of staff and being a patient, she thought as Cherry brought in the tray. Officially, Livvy was supposed to be sitting out in the ward with the rest of them to have her meal, but as the unofficial liaison between the two wards she needed to be in close contact with the telephone and computer links to the rest of the hospital.

'At least we're warm and dry and well fed,' she added cheerfully, breathing in the savoury smells as she lifted up the plate cover.

She caught her breath suddenly as another contraction gripped her, but when she remembered to relax it was fairly easy to weather it. It was all good practice for when the real thing happened.

'Are you all right?' Pat asked with a note of concern in her voice, and Livvy suddenly realised just how sharp-eyed the young staff nurse was.

'Braxton Hick's contractions,' she explained offhand-edly as her breathing returned to normal. 'They've been happening quite strongly for several weeks now. As they're intermittent I never know when to expect them and they sometimes catch me out.'

'You're sure that's what they are?' Pat demanded suspiciously. 'You're not in labour, are you?'

'No such luck.' Livvy laughed. 'I've got two more weeks to go, and knowing my luck, I'll end up carting this lump around right till the last possible minute. I've almost forgotten what it feels like to be able to bend in the middle or catch sight of anything below the Plimsoll line!'

Just then the phone rang and Pat reached out to answer it.

'Maternity. Pat Lersh,' she said, then listened for a minute, her expression growing darker by the second.

'Yes. She's here. I'll pass you over,' she said swiftly, waiting just long enough for Livvy to put her meal aside before she handed her the receiver. 'It's Amy.'

'Livvy here,' she began, but Amy wasn't waiting for social chit-chat.

'Can you come to the delivery suite straight away? I can't get hold of Aled and I've got a problem,' she said succinctly.

'Of course. I'll be with you in...' Livvy stopped speaking when she realised that Amy wasn't listening any more.

The swift cutting of the connection brought home to her just how urgent the matter must be, and that was enough to get her out of her seat and on her feet, pregnant or not.

'See if you can get hold of Daniel,' she suggested, wondering where he'd disappeared to after Nerys's baby had arrived.

Her heart sank at the thought that her attitude towards him in the delivery suite after the Owens baby was born might have made him change his mind about staying around. If, as Amy said, she couldn't get hold of Aled then Daniel was their only hope if there was a mother or baby at risk.

A sudden thought struck her and she called back over her shoulder. 'Check to see if he's gone to get something to eat, or he might be visiting his father up on Orthopaedics.'

Within a couple of minutes Livvy was once more swathed in an ill-fitting gown and pulling on gloves as she reversed through the swing doors.

'Amy,' Livvy called softly when she saw her bending over her patient to speak to her.

'Thank God you're here,' Amy whispered when she'd made her excuses for a second and hurried across to speak to Livvy.'

'I've got a shoulder dystocia and I'm going to need some help. I've assisted several, but I've never had to do one myself. I know the delivery usually needs more than one pair of hands but there's always been an obstetrician in the unit before. I tried external over-rotation of the head but it didn't free it. I can't get it to budge.'

Livvy drew in a breath and released it in a silent whistle of dismay. She would far prefer it if Daniel was to turn up at any second, but they couldn't afford to wait.

Her first glance at the patient had told her that the woman was very overweight, a factor which was often contributory in such cases. She also seemed to be totally alone.

'No partner?' she murmured softly.

'Works away from home and out of contact at the moment. We're all she's got,' Amy replied succinctly. 'I couldn't believe it when the head delivered safely then everything came to a halt. Those shoulders are well and truly stuck. I'm just amazed how calmly she's taking it.'

'OK,' Livvy said, and shrugged her own shoulders right up to her ears and circled them back down again to relax her muscles. 'Let's have a look.'

'This is Jo Moffat,' Amy said, beginning with basic introductions. 'Jo, this is Livvy Jones. She's a midwife and she's going to have a look at you.'

Amy added an aside to Livvy. 'I told Jo that her baby must have Arnold Schwarzenegger's shoulders, and we were having a bit of difficulty turning them to the right position so they can be pushed out.'

'And I told her I hoped that meant it was a boy, 'cos I certainly don't want a girl with Arnie's shoulders,' the patient joked bravely around the Entonox mask.

'Well, we aren't going to find out the sex of the baby until we get that bit out on view,' Livvy pointed out. 'If you'd like to take a couple of deep breaths through the mask to take the edge off the discomfort, I'll just see what I can feel. Whatever you do, don't push.'

'I'll tell you what you'll feel—a quart stuffed into a pint pot,' Jo Moffat grumbled, but she quickly complied with the encouragement to breathe in the gas.

It didn't take long for Livvy to complete her examination, and the only good thing she could see was that the internal presentation seemed to be the same as a couple of previous cases she'd had a hand in delivering—literally.

'The first thing I want to do is get some more pain relief into her so she'll relax,' Livvy muttered softly when she compared findings with Amy, one ear tuned to the way their patient was panting her way through a contraction. 'As soon as I went to examine her she tensed up and we're going to need every millimetre we can get if we're going to pull this cork out of the bottle.'

'We're also going to need a larger episiotomy, aren't we?' Amy asked.

'I've got small hands so we could keep that possibility in reserve,' Livvy suggested. 'I don't like cutting any more than I have to. For now I want to get the analgesic into her and see if we can rotate the baby far enough to get that anterior shoulder out from behind the pubis, without fracturing the clavicle.'

It didn't take much encouragement to get the patient to breathe steadily and deeply to build up the amount of pain relief in her system when Livvy explained what they were going to be doing.

'There isn't room for the *baby* in there,' Jo squeaked in horror. 'How do you think you're going to get your hand in as well?'

'Not my *whole* hand,' Livvy pointed out.

'I bet it'll feel like it,' Jo muttered, and took her first deep breath.

As Livvy prepared to slip her fingers past the baby's vulnerable neck she could hear the echo of Daniel's voice inside her head.

He'd been in the delivery room with her the first time she'd faced a case of shoulder dystocia, and he'd said then that to cope with it you needed either long, strong fingers and a lot of luck or slender agile fingers and a lot of luck.

He'd had the long, strong fingers and she'd had the slender, agile fingers, and between the two of them they'd made an almost unbeatable team.

'Why did this happen?' Jo panted between deep

draughts of gas. 'Is the baby too big? Should I have had a Caesarean?'

'There can be several reasons,' Livvy said, the words interspersed by pauses as she concentrated on what she was doing.

'Usually, as the baby's head starts to come out it will begin to turn so that the shoulders are at the right angle to fit through the space in your pelvis. If that doesn't happen and the baby is coming down the passage fast he can hit a roadblock with his shoulder. With the contractions pushing him from behind, he gets stuck so he can't turn.'

It was difficult to maintain her explanation while she tried to manipulate the wedged baby into a more helpful position. The thing that kept her talking was the fact that she could feel through the pressure on her fingers that when Jo was busy listening, instead of talking, she was breathing in enough gas, and concentrating on Livvy's voice allowed her body to relax.

There was the sound of hushed footsteps behind her and the familiar rustle of a gown. She knew it couldn't be Amy coming towards them—she was standing close by, supporting the baby's head—but it could have been almost anyone else, including Aled Parry or the anaesthetist.

It was the tingle of awareness which travelled through her that told Livvy that Daniel had entered the room and was now standing right behind her.

'How's it going?' he murmured softly, his husky voice sounding strangely intimate in the clinical surroundings.

Livvy closed her eyes as a mixture of relief and pleasure swept through her and kept them closed to force

herself to maintain her concentration. It was amazing
how much more heart his presence had put in her, but
she couldn't afford to be distracted by his nearness.

'It's not…yet!' she muttered briefly through clenched
teeth as she struggled to get just a bit more leverage.
She certainly wasn't ready to call it quits. 'I can't quite
get… Ah! Got it!' she crowed suddenly as something
shifted. 'Now I just need to rotate the shoulder and…
That's enough of the happy gas, Jo. I need you to give
me a big push,' she ordered as she guided the little
shoulder. 'One really big one now.'

It was obviously a relief to the poor woman to be able
to obey her body's instincts again because she complied
willingly.

This time the effort produced movement and, as if
there'd never been a problem, one large baby boy slith-
ered into Livvy's hands and let out an indignant bellow.

'It's Arnold all right,' Amy announced with a burst
of laughter as she took over the care of the baby. 'The
equipment isn't quite the same size yet but it's all there.'

'Delivered through a moderate-sized episiotomy *and*
with no broken clavicle,' Daniel said softly. 'Well done.'

'I'd begun to wonder if we were going to have to push
the head back up and go for a Caesarean,' Livvy admitted quietly. 'I actually gave in and tried to break the
clavicle at one point, but the damn thing wouldn't go.'

'Congratulations on your persistence, then. Yet again
you proved my adage.'

'I'm just glad that I got a lot of the luck to go with
my slender fingers,' Livvy said, letting him know she
remembered what he'd told her.

'Well, I definitely think that success deserves to be

celebrated with a cup of tea,' he announced, and gestured towards the door.

'Sister?' called a voice behind them. 'Wait a minute.'

Livvy turned to see a happily tearful new mum holding her precious son.

'I just wanted to thank you,' she said. 'I know I was joking and everything, but I was so afraid that he was going to die before you got him out.'

'In that case, you should really be thanking Dr Jones here because he's the one who taught me to get that sort of cork out,' Livvy teased lightly. 'He taught me the right way to do it, and also that you don't give up until you've succeeded.'

'In that case, thank you both.' Jo smiled, her eyes glittering with the threat of more tears. 'I've decided I'm going to call him David.'

Livvy knew her smile had dimmed but she had to say something. Was *everyone* calling their son David?

'I've always liked that name,' she said with a lightness she didn't feel. 'I think it will suit him better than Arnold.'

They left the room and Daniel stripped his own disposable gown off then took Livvy's from her.

'It's time you were off your feet,' he announced, and ushered her out to the corridor. 'I saw you wincing when you were up to your elbows on that job so your back's probably killing you.'

'You won't hear me arguing with the prospect of getting my hands on a cup of tea and putting my feet up,' she said, as she revelled in his protective arm around her back.

Self-sufficiency was all very well, but it seemed like years since anyone had taken care of her. Since she'd

known the pleasures of a good partnership it was bliss
to have someone who wanted to make certain that she
put her feet up and... Her happy thoughts ground to a
halt as she realised where they were leading.

There was no point in deluding herself with an impossible happily-ever-after scenario when she'd already
lost him.

In spite of the euphoria of the successful delivery, she
was in a rather more sober frame of mind when he
pushed open the door to the ward.

Unlike Daniel. He seemed positively full of the joys
of...well, hardly spring, with all that snow outside.

It must be the good news that Alice and the baby were
going to be all right. Either that or he'd had good news
about his father.

She turned to ask him if he'd been in contact with the
orthopaedic ward just as they stepped into her own do-
main.

'Hey, Doc. Look up,' called a male voice from about
halfway along the room, obviously one of her ladies'
visitors.

Automatically, Daniel brought the two of them to a
halt just inside the doorway and looked up at the sprig
of green taped to the lintel.

'Good idea,' he called back with a wicked chuckle.
'Can't miss out on a kiss. Bound to be bad luck.' And
before Livvy realised what he intended to do, he'd leant
forward swiftly to brush his lips over hers.

Livvy gasped in horror, her eyes immediately flying
towards Alice Jones's bed.

She was even more horrified to see that she was looking their way and couldn't have missed seeing what
Daniel had done.

# CHAPTER SEVEN

'WHAT do you think you're doing?'

Horrified and embarrassed beyond belief, Livvy tried to extricate herself surreptitiously from Daniel's grasp but he easily prevented it, by tightening his arm around her.

While the infuriating man just laughed down at her from his six-inch height advantage the room filled with a chorus of whistles and cheers, but when it looked as if he was going to do it again Livvy knew she had to call a halt.

'Stop it!' she hissed, and managed to jab him in the ribs with her elbow.

'Oof! What was that for?' he demanded, trying hard to look injured, but Livvy knew he was just playing to the gallery.

'Behave yourself. Alice can see what you're doing,' Livvy said as she hurried towards the office to hide the fierce blush of mortification that heated her cheeks.

'So?' he challenged with another wicked grin as he followed in her wake. 'As far as I know, there's no law against kissing under the mistletoe or half the fun would disappear out of Christmas.'

'But you're married!' she objected, knowing that *she* certainly wouldn't have wanted to see him kissing an ex-wife if their positions had been reversed.

'So?' he repeated. 'Most of the people in the ward are married, too, and as at least half of them are pregnant they weren't seeing anything new. Anyway, as a married man, I can tell you that I heartily approve of kissing, whether under the mistletoe or anywhere else.'

She remembered it well, damn him, Livvy thought as she recalled the heady days of their marriage when he'd found any excuse to practise the art.

But that didn't mean that he could continue now.

'Well, you'll have to learn self-control, then, won't you?' she snapped, turning on him clumsily and blocking his path into the office. There just wasn't enough space in there for her to share with him while he was in this strangely ebullient mood.

What on earth had got into him? Had he had good news about his father?

'Have you checked up on your father yet? I presume he's out of Theatre?'

As a distraction, the topic worked perfectly.

'He's out and has already been taken up to the ward,' he told her, obviously delighted. 'When I visited, they told me he'd been plated and screwed in multitudinous directions to hold everything in position, but the operation had gone well. I was actually able to speak to him for a little while.'

'He was awake enough to speak to you?' Livvy was amazed. His father had probably been under anaesthetic for anything up to four hours—maybe more, depending on the mess the surgeon had found when he'd got in there. 'He must have phenomenal powers of recovery.'

'I think it was fear and guilt that brought him round so soon,' Daniel said soberly. 'He thought he'd killed Davey, Alice and the baby.'

'*He'd* killed them?' Livvy frowned.

'He was the one driving the car when it went out of

control so he blamed himself. When I saw how much
the weather had deteriorated during the ceremony I *did*
offer to play chauffeur but that would have meant one
car having to be retrieved later.'

Livvy didn't quite understand the logistics of the
problem, but it wasn't that important.

'I suppose the BMW was written off in the crash,' she
ventured, mourning the loss of the first car they'd chosen
together—the most luxurious one she'd ever driven in.

'Not at all,' he said with a frown. 'It was Dad's car
that crashed. I was following a little way behind and saw
it happen. I was able to alert the emergency services on
my mobile phone.'

'But…' There was definitely something here that
didn't sound right. 'Why wasn't Alice travelling with
you?'

'That's what I suggested—the BMW's a far more
comfortable car than Dad's old Volvo, but he insisted
that he wanted to drive her to the hotel for the reception
and the baby seat was already strapped in.'

He suddenly clicked his fingers.

'Oh, Lord! I remembered to tell Dad that *she* was all
right but I forgot to tell Alice about Dad's operation,'
he groaned. 'I'm going to find my neck in a noose.'

Before Livvy could say a word he was gone, hurrying
towards Alice's bed.

There was an awful fascination in watching the way
he sat himself down on the edge of the mattress and
cradled one of Alice's hands in his while he spoke earnestly for a moment.

From her vantage point at the end of the ward Livvy
could see his heart-stopping, caring smile as he passed
on the good news to Alice.

It was painful enough to see the two of them together, but it was the way she suddenly wrapped her arms around his neck and pulled him towards her for a heart-felt hug that tied Livvy's throat in a knot and wouldn't let her breathe.

It was just sheer bad timing that made her next Braxton Hicks contraction arrive at that precise moment, and if she'd had enough breath she'd have been hard-pressed not to shout out.

Carefully, she propped her hips against the desk and gripped the edge with white-knuckled hands as she con-centrated, focusing all her thoughts on staying as relaxed as possible while she controlled her breathing.

'Wow, that was the strongest one yet,' she muttered, releasing a deep breath of relief as it began to fade. 'If they're just the practice runs, I'm certainly not looking forward to the real thing.'

She straightened and rested both hands on the full curve of her swollen belly, stroking it gently.

'At least you're being a little quieter at the moment, aren't you, monster? Did someone finally make you un-derstand that you're not supposed to be so energetic by this stage?'

'Uh-oh! She's started talking to the filing cabinet,' Pat teased as she entered the room. 'That kiss must have scrambled her brains completely.'

'Don't mention it, please,' Livvy groaned, embar-rassed all over again. 'Wretched man. Has he forgotten that I have to work here? It'll be all round the hospital in no time and I won't be able to look anyone in the eye.'

'It certainly will be all around the hospital if I have anything to do with it,' Pat confirmed with glee. 'Just wait till I see Sue and Amy. Fancy you working here all this time, without even mentioning that you were hiding someone as gorgeous as him at home. You're a real dark horse.'

'Uh, Pat,' Livvy began, knowing the time had come to explain about the divorce.

In view of her obviously pregnant state, she'd been avoiding any mention of it—after all, what were the chances that any of the staff would ever meet Daniel?

She'd hoped quite desperately that he would have come looking for her when she'd disappeared out of his life, but when even her appearance at his mother's funeral hadn't prompted a visit that hope had died. Especially when she'd seen Alice's arrival at his father's house.

The trouble was, how was she going to tell Pat about her divorce and the circumstances surrounding it, without revealing Alice's part in the events of seven months ago? Could that be termed violating a patient's privacy?

'Actually, Livvy, I came in to ask if you could be persuaded to join the group going round singing,' Pat said, and the moment was lost.

'I've done it a couple of years and thoroughly enjoyed it. Once your little one arrives you probably won't want to take the time away from him or her at Christmas so this might be your last chance. Unless, of course, you can't carry a tune in a bucket and would rather not?'

'I'm certainly not operatic standard,' Livvy admitted honestly. 'I hardly like to put myself forward when my only claim to Welsh tunefulness is my name.'

'Not wanting to be rude, but this year they're desperate enough to be looking for quantity rather than quality. Go on. You'll have fun.'

'But what about the patients? I know I'm not officially on duty but—'

'Don't worry about the ward—I can always get the switchboard to track you down if we need you, and Amy's not much more than a quick shout away in the delivery suite.'

'Oh?' This was news to Livvy. 'Has another one of the upstairs ladies gone into production, then? Do you know which one?'

'I don't know her name but she's another experienced mum who's had the last two as easily as shelling peas. Apparently, she's hoping that she'll be able to go home to the rest of the family in the morning if everything goes smoothly.'

'Sounds like she's a glutton for punishment if she wants to hurry back to running the home that quickly,' Livvy said with a worried frown. 'I hope she's not going to be doing too much too soon or both she and the baby could suffer.'

'It's either that or she doesn't want to miss the baby's first Christmas with the family. We could always make her release conditional that her husband did everything for the next few days,' Pat suggested. 'Anyway, I've always felt that there's something very special about babies born at Christmas, especially those born on Christmas day.'

'It could certainly save a lot on presents,' Livvy pointed out, with her tongue firmly in her cheek. 'They'd be able to have Christmas and birthday all rolled into one.'

'Oh, I don't like that idea,' Pat objected, her expression quite horrified. 'Poor little things would miss out on a special celebration every year.'

A movement at the corner of her eye drew Livvy's attention as Cherry hurried through the doorway, once again quite breathless with excitement.

'Sister? I think that jinx of having babies arriving in bunches is working again,' she announced with shining eyes and a broad grin.

'Uh-oh! Who is it this time?' Pat demanded.

'I'm almost certain Alwyn Morgan's just started labour. I was right beside her when the monitor went off.' Cherry turned to go back to the ward then spun back with words bubbling out of her, her pixie hat flopping wildly.

'I'll admit I wasn't looking forward to being on duty over Christmas because I thought I would be missing out on all the excitement of the celebrations at home, but this has been so much better than I expected. Things have been almost non-stop for hours!' She threw them a final infectious grin and bounced out of the room.

'Were we ever that young and enthusiastic?' Pat demanded in the wake of her departure, and Livvy groaned.

Then they both stayed still and listened, their heads up like animals trying to pinpoint an elusive sound.

At first all that could be heard was the chaotic mixture of noises in the ward, with voices tumbling over each other as they vied for supremacy with the television and Christmas carols.

They smiled simultaneously when they suddenly heard the distinctive electronic sound of the monitor cut through the rest.

'Thank goodness for that,' Pat said, voicing Livvy's equal delight. 'The poor girl was beginning to get very depressed that it was taking so long.'

'Well, it was bad enough, having to be confined to bed for months so she didn't lose the baby,' Livvy pointed out, grateful that there hadn't been any similar problems with her own pregnancy. 'Once the ultrasound confirmed that the baby was fully developed and they took her off the drugs she obviously thought she'd automatically go straight into labour.'

'Perhaps she should have watched Mr Darcy sooner,' Pat joked. 'He obviously got her hormones stirred up and got things moving.'

Livvy chuckled at the idea then heaved herself up off the edge of the desk again, silently groaning at the resulting backache as she started to make for the door.

'Oops! Time for a quick detour to the toilet,' she announced wryly when other pressing needs made themselves known. 'I'll meet you by Alwyn's bed in a few minutes.'

Unlike the last few mums, Alwyn's labour progressed very slowly and steadily, and as none of the others in the ward seemed to be going to start anything interesting Livvy finally made the decision to join the ragtag choir for their trip around the wards.

'Here, you can borrow this cloak,' Amy offered.

Livvy took a closer look at the woman making the offer and saw how tired she looked. It couldn't be easy for her to cope with this level of pressure and responsibility while she was feeling less than a hundred per cent. Livvy could remember vividly how drained she'd felt during the all-day nightmare called morning sickness.

Still, with Alwyn's slow progress the only one to

monitor, perhaps Amy would be able to catch her breath a bit.

Amy had arrived soon after the debris from the meal had been cleared away to report the birth of a rather small but otherwise perfectly healthy baby girl, and found Livvy, preparing to set off.

Now she was holding out one of the traditional heavy nurse's cloaks that was a thick navy fabric on the outside and lined with bright scarlet.

'We usually turn it inside out to give everything an extra Christmassy feel,' Amy said. 'You'll probably find that when you join the rest of them you'll also be given a length of tinsel to put in your hair, like an angel's halo.'

'As long as they don't expect me to sit on top of the Christmas tree,' Livvy warned darkly.

The two of them glanced down at her ungainly shape and burst out laughing at the idea.

The tour was due to begin in the main reception area of the hospital, and there was already a small crowd of porters, Casualty staff and patients gathered as Livvy stepped out of the lift. One of the group was just checking the tuning on his guitar as Livvy nervously walked across to join them.

'Oh, good. Another volunteer,' announced a voice and Livvy felt her face heat furiously when everyone turned to look at her as she scurried to hide herself in the edge of the group.

At least she could console herself that her borrowed cloak went a long way to camouflaging her rather distinctive shape. She doubted they'd ever had a heavily pregnant member in their choir before. Hardly the traditional image of ethereal heavenly hosts…

Amy had been right about the tinsel, too, and Livvy was just trying to use one of her hair clips to get the wretched thing to stay on her head when someone stepped up behind her and it was taken out of her hand.

'Allow me,' said the slightly husky tone of a familiar tenor voice, and she turned to look up into the well-remembered blue of Daniel's eyes.

Silently she relinquished her hold, unable to prevent her fingers brushing his as she handed him the clip. Then she had to stand still while he stood behind her to twine the strands around her head in the form of a coronet.

Just the touch of his fingers against her head while he carefully skewered the strands in position was enough to send shivers of awareness to every extremity.

Her pulse began racing and her skin almost seemed to tingle with the heat she could feel radiating from his body, so that all she could think about was how close he was standing. It didn't help that he didn't say another word, making absolutely no effort to break the silent cocoon that seemed to surround them.

When he'd finished the task she managed to find her voice to thank him, but when she would have moved away to put some distance between them he caught her elbow and drew her attention to the small sheaf of papers he retrieved from his pocket.

'I've got the words of all the songs so you'd better stay with me to share,' he suggested. His advice was logical enough but the expression in his eyes carried more than a hint of challenge.

Livvy didn't know if she was up to it, not with her emotions in such turmoil after the events of the last twelve hours.

With the memories of a similar event last year so clear

in her head she didn't know if she could endure a whole evening with their heads bent together over the same sheet of paper, and she glanced around for some reasonable form of escape. When she realised that the majority of the choir had already paired up she was left with little alternative but to agree.

She didn't voice her reservations but he must have known, otherwise why did his actions seem so deliberate when he made concentration so difficult by pressing his shoulder so closely to hers?

Then, when he changed sides and wrapped his free arm around her waist, she honestly didn't know whether to give up the attempt at singing and go back to the ward or simply wallow in the unexpected guilty pleasure.

It was all so much like Christmas Eve a year ago that she didn't know whether to laugh or cry.

For a while, as they worked their way through the repertoire of songs and moved their way from ward to ward, Daniel was able to concentrate on his singing.

When they'd started off in the children's wards with 'Rudolph the Red-Nosed Reindeer' and 'Jingle Bells' he'd been afraid that she was going to insist on treating him the same as any other member of the choir. He'd been reduced to deliberately using his possession of the song sheet as an excuse to stand close to her.

It didn't take long before he recognised from the raised colour in her cheeks that his ploy was working, that she'd been forced to acknowledge his physical presence beside her, and he stepped up his campaign by curving one arm around her.

He tried to do it casually so that she wouldn't balk at the implied intimacy, but inside he yearned for her to accept the gesture as it was really meant—that she could use his body as a source of comfort and support the way she had a year ago.

Unfortunately for his peace of mind, as the evening wore on her proximity began to have its usual effect on him and he found himself less and less able to control his response to the woman beside him.

After seven months of separation, having his arm around her was like offering a sip of water to a man dying of thirst.

At first he tried to blame his discomfort on the elusive flowery scent that wafted over him whenever they leaned closer to read the words of unfamiliar verses.

He had no idea what it was called, but it was one that would always remind him of the steamy air she'd left behind when she'd finished in the bathroom.

Most of all it would remind him of the way his own skin had smelled when he'd joined her in the shower and wrapped himself around her slick, soapy body. He glanced sideways at that body, hidden now under the tent-like structure of her nurse's cloak.

From his observations today of her shape and the way she was moving he was pretty certain that she was close to full term, and that would mean... He did a quick mental calculation and felt a reminiscent smile cover his face. If his mathematics was correct, he had a damn good idea exactly when that baby she was carrying had been conceived.

His body reacted predictably when he remembered that it was just such an occasion in the shower that could have been the culprit.

After several days when their shifts had left them with little time together he'd made a special effort and had actually been able to leave the hospital on time, knowing that they'd been invited out that evening.

He'd arrived home with time to spare and had surprised her in the bathroom, getting ready to go out to their colleagues' engagement party.

No matter how stern he was with himself while he stood surrounded by a dozen or so complete strangers he couldn't help the mental images unrolling in his mind like an X-rated film as he remembered the alternative way that evening had been spent.

Without saying a word to alert her that he was there, he'd stripped his own clothes off his heavily aroused body and had joined her behind the recently installed opaque glass screen.

Her eyes had been tightly closed against the sting of shampoo and she'd squealed with shock when he'd wrapped his arms around her slender body and pulled her against him from head to toe to possess her with a ravenous kiss.

The body leaning against him now wasn't the same slender one he remembered from that memorable night, but somehow the full, blatantly fertile curves she'd developed since then only served to attract him more. Until he'd seen her body shaped by his baby growing inside her, he hadn't realised how much he'd wanted to see her this way.

He had to pause in his singing to clear his throat, amazed and horrified to realise that his thoughts had actually brought him to full arousal.

Was he some sort of pervert, for heaven's sake, to be lusting like this after a heavily pregnant woman?

No, he decided resolutely, he was just a man attracted

to a woman regardless of her physical appearance...or was it that?

He cast her several sidelong glances before he shook his head firmly.

No. In Livvy's case he was attracted to her because she was Livvy. Whether she had the figure of a slender sprite or the quintessential earth mother was immaterial.

He drew in the next breath to continue singing 'Once in Royal David's City' and sighed heavily instead.

He certainly hadn't expected to be pitchforked into this sort of situation when he'd decided to confront Livvy. He needed to talk to her but with the siege atmosphere in the hospital it had been all too easy for her to avoid him.

He pressed his lips together when he thought about how badly he must have hurt her.

He couldn't believe that she'd moved so far away—to Wales, for heaven's sake. It was hours by road from St Augustine's and almost impossible by train.

The only reason he could think of was that the idiot woman had chosen to move here in the belief that a Jones would be able to disappear for ever in a country full of Joneses. And, because he hadn't been in contact with her in the months that had passed since she came here, she must have convinced herself that he didn't care enough about her to look very hard.

He had a horrible feeling that it was going to be an uphill task to persuade her otherwise.

The fact that he'd finally tracked Livvy to this hospital at the same time as he was in the middle of organising the wedding nearby had seemed the height of serendipity. The location had been suggested by his father so that they could combine it with a visit to their few surviving relatives—those same relatives who hadn't even been invited when he'd married Livvy because he couldn't bear to wait to make her his.

As soon as the ceremony was over this morning he'd had every intention of asking Alice to release him from his promise and then he'd be free to search Livvy out and make his long-overdue explanations.

What a fool he'd been to allow Alice to come between him and Libby. He'd known all along that his blonde-haired sprite was the best thing to have happened in his life and he'd been stupid enough to give someone else the power to spoil it.

Well, enough was enough.

He loved Livvy as much as ever and wanted her back—*needed* her back in his life or it wasn't worth living.

He'd spoken to Alice to pass on the good news about Davey and his father's operation and at the same time had told her his decision. He'd deliberately left her little option, but she'd finally agreed to release him from his promise.

Now all he had to do was persuade Livvy to hear him out and he might stand a chance of getting his life back on track. He wasn't going to let himself think about the possibility that he'd lost her trust for ever. That was a prospect that had kept him awake for more nights than he cared to think about.

There was just one more ward to visit after this, the obstetrics ward that Livvy had been spending most of her time in today, and then—

Suddenly, the guitarist began to play the plaintively simple introduction to 'Silent Night' and Daniel's heart turned over.

Instantly he was surrounded by the magic memories of a year ago when the two of them had taken part in a very similar Christmas Eve's tradition at St Augustine's.

Then, as now, they'd been standing in a ward full of mothers and babies, both those already born and those still in waiting, as they'd gathered for the impromptu concert.

Then, as now, he'd had his arm round her shoulders as they'd shared the song sheet.

He hadn't realised until then just how beautifully the tone of her voice blended with his, and when he'd begun to sing the harmony to her melody their voices had blended and twined so seamlessly that it had been enough to draw the soul out of his body. If only that harmony could once more extend into their lives as well.

For just a moment when the familiar notes sounded he'd felt her stiffen within the circle of his arm and knew that she was remembering too. But then she relaxed again and when they began to sing it sounded to his hopeful ears as if she was letting the words and music come from her heart.

Livvy could feel the tremor in her voice as she joined in with the familiar words of the first verse of 'Silent Night', the memories sharp enough to cut her like a knife. But suddenly it was as if the last year had disappeared and all she knew was that she and Daniel were together, their voices blending effortlessly.

She was so wrapped up in the song that she didn't see Daniel make any signal but when the second verse began and she realised that theirs were the only voices left singing, she faltered. Her eyes flew up to his as uncertainty struck, but when she met his steady blue gaze and realised that he was willing her to continue what else could she do?

Once more he sang the harmony to her melody, the simple tune taking on an unearthly poignance in the quiet of the dimly lit ward.

She barely noticed that the rest of the choir joined in for the final verse, her heart too full of the realisation that one song could be the focus of everything that had changed in her life. Since the last time they'd sung it together she'd become pregnant and carried the child to within a few days of term, but she'd lost the man who had fathered that child.

She might try to tell herself that she couldn't keep looking back over her shoulder, that she must move on with her life, but with his clear blue eyes fixed intently on hers she had to admit to herself that he was the only man she would ever love.

The carol came to an end and after several seconds of appreciative silence there was a swift burst of applause.

At first Livvy was oblivious to it all, with Daniel smiling down at her and holding her snugly at his side as though she belonged there.

Suddenly Livvy couldn't take any more.

'Excuse me,' she whispered, taking him by surprise when she turned away as swiftly as her ungainly shape would allow and broke his hold on her. 'I've got to go.'

A group of patients was converging on their little choir with smiles and words of praise but she couldn't bear to stay, taking advantage of the temporary mêlée to make her escape.

# CHAPTER EIGHT

'LIVVY, wait!'

The sound of Daniel's voice, following her along the corridor, was enough to lend wings to her feet.

In spite of the fact that her traitorous body decided to try to break her in half with another clenching spasm of pain she forced her feet to move a little faster.

She knew it was going to take him a few minutes to fight his way out of the surrounding throng but he could move so much more quickly than she could. It wouldn't take him long to catch her up.

The lift doors closed behind her with a soft sigh and she gave a sigh of her own as she leaned gratefully against the antiseptic-smelling wall and waited to be delivered to the floor below.

Heat surged up into her face when she thought about the spectacle she'd made of herself just now. She'd been tricked into partnering her less-than-perfect voice with Daniel's for that impromptu duet in front of all those people. Heaven knew, that was embarrassing enough when she thought that she was going to have to face all her colleagues within the department, knowing they'd heard her make a fool of herself.

It was all very well Daniel trying to tell her that she had a lovely voice, but she knew he was just being kind. Her mother had been the one with the voice in their family and she knew she could never compare.

The worst part was knowing that everyone on the

ward and in the choir had been watching the two of them, and when she'd looked up at him they must have been able to see the besotted expression on her face. What made it worse was that once she'd met his gaze she hadn't been able to help herself.

Once they'd started singing that carol her brain seemed to have switched to automatic pilot, completely ignoring the fact that she was no longer married to the man. When she'd seen the warmth in his eyes she'd been helpless and unable to look away.

There was a soft jolt as the lift arrived and she stepped out into the corridor, the contraction beginning to die away now.

As she unfastened the ties of the borrowed cloak and slid it off her shoulders her feet automatically took her towards the ward. After all, she thought wryly, where else could she go?

It was Christmas Eve and outside was the perfect illustration for a million Christmas cards, with the snow lying deep and crisp and even.

Knowing the narrow road that led to her cottage, there was no way she would be able to get there by taxi, and she wasn't exactly in the right physical shape to walk the distance even if a taxi driver could be persuaded to take her as far as the end of her turning.

As she folded the heavy cloak over her arm tiredness suddenly overwhelmed her and she had a mental image of the hospital bed reserved for her on the ward.

What a relief it would be to curl up under crisp sheets and shut her brain down for the night. It was all very well wanting to keep her hands and mind occupied to stave off boredom, but eventually she was going to have to admit that a nearly-nine-months pregnant woman just didn't have the same reserves of energy.

As she pushed the ward door open all eyes turned towards her and she suddenly remembered that the choir still had to come here to sing.

'They're here!' called Megan Williams as she settled herself back against a bank of pillows with her precious daughter cradled in her arms.

'They're on their way,' Livvy corrected, while her brain frantically tried to think of somewhere to hide out until it was all over. She could hardly spend the next half hour in the bathroom or someone would come looking for her, thinking she was in labour.

'All that standing around was killing me so I ducked out,' she added by way of explanation.

'Oh, Sister,' breathed Cherry in obvious relief as her head popped around the corner from Sister's office. 'I was hoping it was your voice I heard. I've been trying to track you down.'

Livvy silenced a groan and straightened her shoulders.

'What did you want? There aren't any problems, are there?'

She glanced quickly around the ward but everyone seemed to be happily waiting for the choir to arrive.

'It's Mrs Morgan—you know, the one on the monitor,' Cherry said, nodding towards the far corner. Livvy suddenly noticed that the young woman wasn't there any more and neither was her tinsel-decorated box of technology. 'Pat was keeping an eye on her and now she's taken her along to the labour suite. She asked me to get hold of you and send you along.'

'Are you all right here?' Livvy demanded, worried that she was leaving such a novice in nominal charge of the ward, but her brain was already whirling with all the potential problems that could be happening in the labour suite.

Alwyn Morgan's labour had been progressing slowly when she'd left the ward but there'd been nothing to worry about on that score. Had something gone wrong?

'Provided no one gets so excited, listening to the choir that they instantly jump to second-stage labour I'll be all right,' the younger woman said with quiet assurance. 'Anyway, I can always shout for help, can't I?'

'Good girl,' Livvy said with a tired smile, appreciating the youngster's steady confidence. 'I've got a feeling you're going to do well on this ward.'

She hurried towards the labour suite, taking with her the memory of the glow of pride that had lit the young nurse's face.

'I felt like that, too, once upon a time,' she muttered, scowling along a corridor that seemed to stretch into infinity. 'About a million years ago before I started carrying an elephant around as a fashion statement.'

'Talking to yourself is supposed to be the first sign of madness,' Pat commented through her smile of relief when Livvy came through the door.

'I've moved on from there to full-blown paranoia,' Livvy informed her grimly as she fought with ties that barely met around her middle. 'I've started answering myself, too.'

A sudden sound made her look up and she met the eyes of the understandably nervous expectant father who now looked quite horrified.

For a moment she was hard-pressed not to laugh aloud but she wasn't certain that she would be able to stop if she did, and that would probably have sent him over the edge too.

It was all very well for hospital staff to joke among themselves that they had to be mad to work here, but when you were waiting for expert help for your wife, you obviously didn't want to know that.

'Don't worry, Mr Morgan,' she said calmly. 'It's the night before Christmas and everyone's allowed to talk a bit of nonsense.'

He tried to find a smile but it was a weak one.

'Now, Pat,' Livvy said in an undertone as she joined her on the other side of the monitor. 'What's the problem?'

'Mum seems fine, but I'm beginning to get worried about the baby,' Pat admitted. 'Each time she has a contraction the baby's pulse drops. For the last half hour it's been a steady downward graph.'

Without having to make a list, Livvy knew there could be several reasons for those findings. Some pointed to danger for the baby and some to danger for mother *and* baby, but none of them were good.

'Have you managed to get hold of anyone?' she asked while the possibility of a hasty Caesarean section loomed large in her mind.

'I paged Aled Parry and he was here within a quarter of an hour, but when he got here he looked more dead than alive so I sent him away again,' Pat said, her more than professional concern for the reserved resident obvious even over her concern for her patients.

'I know he's only just recovering from that flu bug and I told him earlier that he sounded dreadful,' Livvy agreed.

'With Duncan French's broken arm putting him out

of commission, and Simon away on holiday and uncontactable, Aled was intending to work straight through the forty-eight hours of Christmas.'

'That's taking devotion to duty rather too far when he's not well himself,' Livvy said. 'Especially when we've got a well-qualified captive replacement available.'

She sent up a mental sigh of resignation as she lumbered heavily across to the phone.

She'd been hoping to keep out of Daniel's way as much as possible for the next twelve hours while keeping her fingers crossed that Alice would be ready to be released tomorrow. Now she was going to have to search him out and ask him to cast a professional eye over yet another patient.

'Obstetrics. Cherry Watts speaking,' said the voice in her ear, and before Livvy could say a word she heard the sound of voices in the background raised in song.

That answered her first question—the choir had arrived.

'It's Livvy Jones here, Cherry. Is Dr Jones with the choir?'

'Yes. Well, no. He arrived on the ward with them, but he's not with the choir exactly,' she floundered.

'Damn. Where's he gone, wretched man?' Livvy muttered as she heard a scuffling sound on the other end of the line.

'And I love you too,' Daniel quipped, the sudden sound of his voice in her ear nearly causing her to drop the receiver. 'Do I take it you want me?'

She could hear the laughter in Daniel's voice but she wasn't smiling.

Yes, she wanted him—would always want him—but that didn't mean she could have him.

'I've got a patient here I'd like you to have a look at,' she announced, trying to ignore his suggestive words. 'Foetal pulse and b.p. dropping,' she added cryptically in case the parents were listening.

'I'll be with you in a minute,' he said briskly, suddenly all business, and the line went dead.

Livvy turned back to the other occupants of the room and this time, with the major weight of the patient's welfare lifted off her shoulders, her smile was genuine.

'Please, Nurse, what's going on?' young Mr Morgan asked as he held his wife's hand in a vice-like grip. 'I can see the numbers for the baby are getting lower. Does that mean he's dying?'

Livvy's heart clenched with dismay. Did he really think that they would stand by idly while his baby slowly died? Sometimes ignorance could be very cruel and the only remedy for that was to explain a little of what was happening. She would keep it simple, knowing that too much information could be just as frightening.

'The numbers you're watching on the monitor are telling us that each time Alwyn has a contraction the baby's blood pressure is going down a bit and his heartbeat slows.'

'Is that dangerous?' demanded Alwyn, her eyes huge in her face. 'It must be or you wouldn't be worried about it, would you?'

'It *could* be dangerous if we didn't check why it was happening and do something about it,' Livvy confirmed. 'As it is, Dr Jones will be here any minute to check things over. He's an obstetrician and gynaecologist, the same as Duncan French.'

'Is he good?' demanded Mr Morgan, and Pat chuckled.

'Good enough to marry,' she said with a grin. 'He's Sister's husband, too, so she knows him well.'

Now was not the time to correct Pat about her marital status— she certainly couldn't do it in front of worried parents-to-be—but soon she was going to have to set her colleague straight.

Anyway, at that moment Livvy heard the swing doors open and she looked up just in time to see Daniel enter the room.

Not wanting to stand too close, she retreated from Alwyn Morgan's side and stood against the wall, gratefully leaning back to try to relieve the nagging ache in her back. She watched Daniel's easy manner as he greeted the frightened couple, knowing that he could set their minds at rest if anyone could.

He accepted Alwyn's notes from Pat and slowly read the résumé of all the problems she'd had over the last two years.

Livvy knew the file started with the two miscarriages she'd endured at about the ten-week mark. When this, her third pregnancy, threatened to go the same way six months ago she'd been brought into hospital for correction of a diagnosed progesterone deficiency and monitoring.

While he was reading, Alwyn had another contraction and Livvy saw him add the latest read-out figures from the foetal monitor to the file.

He put the notes to one side without comment and turned to Alwyn to begin a thorough examination, taking the time to explain at each stage what he was looking

for and why and always keeping his explanations clear
and simple.

When he eventually straightened and stood frowning
for a moment, Livvy wasn't in the least surprised that
neither Alwyn nor her husband interrupted his thoughts.
They had obviously decided to trust the man implicitly
in spite of the fact that they barely knew him.

She remembered the feeling well.

Right from the first time she'd met Daniel, when
they'd survived their collision in the corridor, she'd
known that he was going to be something special in her
life—she'd never have agreed to marry him so quickly
if that hadn't been the case.

She had known him for just a few weeks before she
had taken a chance, trusting him enough to place her
heart in his keeping.

Shelving the painful memories of the way he had broken that trust, Livvy forced herself to concentrate on the
situation in front of her.

During his examination of Alwyn she had realised that
Daniel had virtually ruled out the possibility of a de-
tached placenta because Alwyn's blood pressure remained within normal bounds. If she had been haemor-
rhaging that would have been a different story.

'I think we've got two possibilities,' he announced at
last, carefully including the baby's parents in the discussion. 'Either the cord's got itself somewhere it
shouldn't so that every time there's a contraction it gets
squeezed and starves the baby of blood or your little
one's just getting tired of the labour taking so long.'

'Can you do anything—speed it up, perhaps?' Tom
Morgan demanded bluntly, and Livvy couldn't help but
admire his determination.

'What I propose doing is keeping an eye on Alwyn and monitoring her closely through the next few contractions. If the blood pressure doesn't drop any further then we can assume that the baby's holding his own. If that's the case, and providing everything doesn't take too long, labour can continue normally.'

'And if it doesn't?' Alwyn prompted, one hand resting protectively on the covered mound that hid her baby.

'If the blood pressure continues to fall then we might not have time to wait for a normal labour. We might have to get the baby out by the quick route.'

'You mean operate?' Tom Morgan asked, his voice rather unsteady at the prospect.

'At this stage it's just a possibility,' Daniel said. 'Whatever happens, we don't want the baby to be at risk. You've both gone through too much to get this far for us to take any chances now.'

The young father turned to his wife and they shared a wordless communication for several long seconds before he turned back to face Daniel.

'OK,' he said simply. 'We trust you to keep the baby safe.'

For a moment Livvy had to blink rapidly to clear the sudden threat of tears from her eyes. It was a testament to Daniel's obvious honesty and concern that the young couple had so readily placed the life of their precious child in his hands.

She tried to straighten away from the wall and when she was suddenly gripped by another pain she couldn't help gasping aloud.

All eyes were turned on her as she tried to control her breathing and the pain.

'What's the matter?' Daniel demanded as he strode

towards her, his straight brows drawn down fiercely over his nose. 'You've been on your feet far too long, you silly woman.'

'Stop fussing,' she hissed between gritted teeth, hating the fact that she wasn't coping very well while he was watching. 'It's just a Braxton Hicks contraction.'

'She had another one earlier,' Pat volunteered.

'How much earlier?' Daniel demanded, one lean hand now resting on Livvy's belly to monitor the progress of the contraction.

'Several hours ago—sometime this morning,' Pat supplied, and Livvy didn't correct her. There had been several in the interim, but if she told Daniel that he'd probably jump to the conclusion that she was in labour and handcuff her to a bed.

'How long until she's full term?' he asked, once more directing his question to Pat.

'Still several weeks yet,' Pat told him, and Livvy gave a mental sigh of relief when he nodded his acceptance. If he'd known that it was now just under two weeks she had a good idea that there was no way he would let her out of his sight until either Aled Parry or Duncan French were fit for duty again or Simon was back from his holiday. He certainly wouldn't be letting her help out on the ward no matter how short of staff they were.

She drew in a deep breath as the contraction faded and slowly became aware that his hand was still resting on the full curve of her belly.

Once it was obvious that the pain had gone she expected him to take his hand away and turn back to their patient, but he didn't move away, standing quite still in front of her.

'Daniel?' She looked up at him, feeling a frown pleating her forehead when she found him staring at his fingers curved over the front of her smock.

She could feel the heat of his hand travelling through the layers of material to reach her tautly stretched skin, and when his fingers spread as if he was trying to encompass the child within, she looked up, needing to see his face to try to divine his thoughts.

Her breath caught in her throat when she saw the expression in his eyes. He looked so sad and suddenly she knew that he must be thinking about how much he had already missed of his baby's life.

As if he'd just noticed where his hand was resting, he abruptly snatched it away and grasped her firmly by the elbow instead.

'You'll be all right in here until I can get this woman off her feet, won't you?' he asked Pat as he started to lead Livvy to the door, pausing just long enough to strip off their disposables with practised efficiency.

'No problem,' Pat agreed with a wry lift of an eyebrow for Livvy when she briefly met her eyes.

'You don't want two of them producing in here at once,' said Tom Morgan, obviously much chirpier now he understood what was going on with his wife.

Livvy objected to having decisions made for her like that and wasn't very keen on being manhandled along the corridor, but as the ultimate object was to get her to relax a bit and as she *was* feeling a bit the worse for wear it wasn't worthwhile saying a word.

Daniel paused for a moment when they entered the ward, finding several members of the choir standing in a knot making their last farewells as they admired the new babies.

Changing direction, he led her towards Sister's office and drew her to a halt beside the desk.

'Tea? Coffee? Water?' he asked, one hand reaching out to check the level of water in the kettle before he switched it on.

'There should be some juice left in the fridge,' Livvy said as she perched on the edge of the desk and surreptitiously tried to rub the ache in her back.

She watched him crouch down in front of the compact fridge to find the container, the muscles bunching in his thighs reminding her of the first time she'd seen them naked. Well, if you could call caked in mud on a rugby pitch naked, she amended. Because he was nearly six feet tall he had long legs but his choice of sport meant that his whole body was well muscled and fit.

He straightened easily and she was forced to drag her eyes away quickly in case he turned and caught her ogling him.

'Were you very sick?' he asked suddenly, the question seeming to come from nowhere as he stood facing her across the room. He appeared to have completely forgotten the carton of orange in his hand as he gazed intently at her.

'Morning, noon and night,' she admitted with a grimace. 'I couldn't stand the smell of bacon or cigarettes—still can't—and I couldn't bear the taste of coffee.'

'That must have made waking up in the morning a problem,' he teased, his expression lightening as he referred to her former habit of setting the coffee-maker on a timer before she went to bed so that it was ready for her first thing.

'Luckily, once I got to three months I could have the

odd cup again but only if it was heavily diluted with milk.'

'What about now?'

'About the same—that's why I've switched to juice or milk. I'm hoping my taste buds will go back to normal once the baby's arrived—at least when I stop breast feeding.'

It had been a throw-away comment but when his eyes suddenly focused on the relevant portion of her anatomy it was as if he'd reached out and touched her.

Livvy felt her nipples react to the visual stimulation and as they were so sensitive these days, anyway, just the friction of her plain cotton maternity bra made them feel as if he'd caressed them through the finest silk.

Afraid that he might notice the physical evidence of her reaction, she tried to disguise it by folding her arms nonchalantly but only succeeded in pulling her smock tight and making her condition look more obvious.

It wasn't as if there was anywhere for her to put her folded arms, with the newly lush curves of her enlarged breasts almost meeting the top of her bulge.

She huffed out an exasperated breath.

'I'll be so glad when this is all over,' she grumbled uncomfortably, remembering how he used to enjoy stroking her and praising her dancer's legs and slender body.

His blonde haired-sprite he used to call her... There wasn't anything very sprightly about her now.

'I didn't realise how clumsy and ungainly I would end up,' she said almost apologetically, suddenly realising just how much her body had changed since he'd last seen her. 'I feel like one of those hot-air balloons, only twice as large and ten times as heavy.'

'You're beautiful,' he exclaimed huskily, his eyes still roaming over her from head to foot, almost as if he was eager to discover her new shape. He seemed especially fascinated by the full curves so poorly disguised under her smock.

She made a wordless sound of denial even as her eyes widened in surprise when she saw the tide of dark colour wash over his cheeks.

He glanced down and didn't seem to know why he had the carton of juice in his hand. He passed it from one hand to the other, focusing on it intently as if he needed something to occupy his hands while he came to a decision.

Suddenly he looked up at her again with a new determination in his expression.

Almost absent-mindedly he put the carton aside and took the half-dozen paces that brought him in front of her.

'You are, you know,' he said earnestly, softly, his hands hovering for a moment before he placed them gently on her shoulders. 'I don't think I've ever seen your skin more radiant or your face more serene. You almost glow with it.'

'Daniel...' She didn't really know what to say. He seemed so sincere, as if he really cared about her, but if that was the case, why had he—

'Oh, Livvy, I've missed you,' he whispered, his voice huskier than ever as he angled his head and brought his lips to meet hers.

For a moment Livvy was transfixed by the heated awareness that flashed through her at the contact.

Helpless to resist when it was what she'd been craving for seven long months, she found herself parting her own lips to admit his sleekly questing tongue and instantly met it in a dark, hidden duel.

She felt more than heard his rough groan of appreciation as it rumbled from his body into hers, and she slid her hands up his arms and over his shoulders to clasp them in the thick softness of his hair in her need to deepen the kiss.

She was completely oblivious to her surroundings, her senses aware only of the fact that she was once again paired with the other half of her soul when he pulled her up from the edge of the desk and into his arms.

The sudden crushing pressure of her pregnant body against his lean strength was shocking in its impact and she wrenched herself away from him.

'Daniel!' she gasped breathlessly as guilt poured through her to dampen her desire. 'We...we shouldn't be doing this. It...it isn't right!'

'I admit it isn't quite as easy as it was when there were just the two of us to consider,' he said teasingly, his voice gravelly with arousal as he glanced down at the protrusion beneath her smock.

'That's just the point,' she snapped, wishing she could just abandon all her principles. How could anything that felt so right be so wrong? 'It's not the two of us any more. There's Alice to consider.'

'Alice?' he repeated with an absent frown as he tried to gather her close again, his eyes intent on her lips. 'What on earth has she got to do with anything?'

'What has she...?' Livvy shook her head in disbelief, trying to ignore the way her whole body was throbbing with denial. It would be so easy to give in to what Daniel wanted because she wanted it too. The trouble was, she wouldn't be able to live with herself afterwards.

'Daniel, what's happened to you?' she demanded as she braced her hands against his chest and glared up at him. 'You used to believe that it was a mark of a man that he kept his word, but in the last seven months you seem to have done nothing but break it, first to me and now with Alice.'

His head came up in surprise and he blinked as if he were surfacing from a deep dive.

'What are you talking about, Livvy?' he demanded, clearly confused. 'What on earth has *Alice* got to do with anything between *us*?'

Livvy drew in a deep breath and started again.

'Daniel, you're a married man and you made certain promises,' she began, only to have him interrupt almost immediately.

'I remember vividly,' he agreed, with a wicked gleam in his eyes. 'I promised to love you and honour you and worship you with my body.'

He reached for her again, his head tilting and his lips already parted in anticipation as they approached hers.

'But that was before the divorce,' she whimpered, as she fought the need to give in to the pleasure she knew he was offering. 'You're not free to love me any more.'

He stopped moving, seemingly turned to stone as he stared at her in stupefaction.

'Divorce?' he repeated in disbelief. 'What divorce?'

'Our divorce,' she said, trying to sound firm. 'The one you had to get before you could marry Alice this morning—unless you're into bigamy.'

The silence seemed to go on for ever as he gazed at her, his eyes boring right through to her soul.

To her utter mortification he suddenly threw his head back and roared with laughter.

'Marry Alice!' he exclaimed, having difficulty saying the words because he was laughing so hard. 'I couldn't marry Alice if I wanted to because I'm still married to you.'

# CHAPTER NINE

LIVVY stared at Daniel, hurt beyond belief that he could be treating the situation so lightly.

'Daniel, she told me herself,' she pointed out, furious that she couldn't control the quiver in her voice and the tremble of her lips. 'You were there and you certainly didn't contradict her.'

'What? When?' he demanded, clearly shocked. That had certainly wiped the laughter off his face.

'When you brought her up to the ward this morning,' she reminded him, the scene all too vivid in her memory because that had been the moment when all her dreams of happiness had died. 'She showed me her ring and told me she was Mrs Jones now. She said you were married this morning.'

'Oh, Livvy, no. You misunderstood what she was saying,' he began, with a horrified expression on his face, only to be interrupted by the phone.

He paused to glare at it, obviously wanting to continue the explanation now that he'd started, but the ringing was imperative and he was forced to turn away, cursing in an exasperated mutter as she reached out to silence the noise.

She knew how he felt.

How could she possibly concentrate on a telephone call when her whole future might be hanging on a thread? How could the whole world not go into suspended animation to give Daniel and herself time to—?

'Livvy, it's Pat. Is Daniel there?'

As soon as she heard the urgent tone of Pat's voice she knew that her own problems were going to have to wait.

'Not good?' she asked.

'Getting rapidly worse,' Pat confirmed succinctly, her voice low-toned enough to tell Livvy that she was trying not to let the young couple overhear her talking. The pregnancy had been a nightmare for them almost from the beginning and they'd weathered it very bravely. It would be heartbreaking if anything went wrong at this stage.

'He's right here. I'll hand you over,' Livvy said and twisted clumsily to hold the receiver out to Daniel.

'It's Pat. The baby's not doing well,' she warned him, then stood with her hands clenched as she listened to his rapid-fire questions.

She didn't need to hear the answers to know what he was hearing. All she had to see was the rapidly darkening expression on his face.

Putting aside her own feelings of sympathy for the young couple, she deliberately switched her brain to thinking about what needed doing. If Daniel had been on the staff here he would have known all the channels. As it was, she was going to be his link between what needed doing and how to achieve it.

By the time he'd put the phone down she'd composed a mental list.

'Caesarean?' she asked, almost certain of the answer.

'Labour has speeded up nicely but the baby's pulse rate is going down alarmingly. How do I get hold of that anaesthetist?'

Livvy's hand was already reaching for the phone. She

knew from what Amy had said that Antonio was staying on call for the duration as well. As the phone began to ring she crossed her fingers childishly and sent up a little prayer that he wasn't already involved in an operation.

'I'll be in the delivery suite,' Daniel said, just as the click at the other end told her the call had been answered. She held up a hand to signal that she'd heard him.

She glanced over her shoulder just in time to cast a longing look at him as he went striding out of the door, and felt a pang of frustration.

They'd been in the middle of one of the most important conversations of her life when all this had blown up in their faces. How long would it be before they could finish?

'Aldarini,' said the voice in her ear as Antonio answered his pager, and instantly her brain switched into work mode.

It took less than five minutes before she put the phone down for the last time and hurried out of the room to deliver her messages in person.

'All arranged,' she announced in quiet triumph as she stuck her head through the swing doors.

Daniel was standing by Alwyn's side, speaking softly to the young woman and her husband, and she knew that he would have spent the time she'd been making her calls explaining what he was going to do and trying to reassure them of their baby's safety.

Livvy just had time to notice that he'd taken hold of the young woman's free hand and patted it gently before he made his excuses and came across to her.

'What have you got?' he demanded briefly, his tension showing in his slightly clipped tone.

'I've got a fully equipped and fully staffed theatre free right now and the anaesthetist is already on his way up to join you there.' Livvy grinned, pleased with the success of her efforts.

'Brilliant!' he said, with relief in his answering grin, and he suddenly leaned forward to bracket her face between his palms and deliver a brief but noisy kiss.

'Daniel!' she squeaked breathlessly over the sudden thundering of her pulse.

'You deserved it for getting everything organised so quickly,' he said unrepentantly, a wicked gleam in his eyes.

'Well, damn!' said Pat with a laugh. 'If I'd known there was a reward like that in the offing I'd have made the phone calls myself!'

Livvy was laughing at Pat's nonsense as she made her way back to the ward but her lips were still tingling from their contact with Daniel's.

Wretched man. It wasn't fair to do things like that when they hadn't finished their discussion.

She had to admit that her heart was immeasurably lighter, though, because, in spite of seven months of pain and disillusionment, deep down she'd discovered that she still trusted him. She'd known from the first that he was a man of honour and integrity so how had everything got in such a mess?

Was it all her fault for not trusting him implicitly? His, for not being open enough to explain what was going on? Both?

She sighed heavily and tried to reach back with both hands to massage the ache that had been gripping her back at intervals all day. She was beginning to feel very tired and very old, especially with all these Braxton

Hicks contractions. She hadn't realised they were going to happen so frequently or be so painful.

The next two weeks weren't going to be much of a picnic if things were going to continue this way—it already felt as if she'd been pregnant for a couple of years.

As she entered the softly lit ward she noticed that most of the patients had settled themselves in their beds to sleep or read with their nightlights on. There were just a few hardy souls left gathered round the low murmur of the flickering television set.

She glanced at the watch pinned to the front of her smock and saw with surprise that it was already ten o'clock. Where had the day gone? Christmas Eve was almost over and Christmas Day would soon be here.

Still rubbing at her back, she wandered across to the window and pulled a corner of the curtain just far enough to see outside.

The sky was mid-winter dark but the layer of snow on the ground lent everything an unearthly glow. Usually the Mynydd Du, the Black Mountains, were completely invisible at night, disappearing into the darkness, but tonight was different.

It had stopped snowing at last and the sky had cleared just far enough to allow the moon to appear. Its soft radiance was reflected back from the snow-covered crags and peaks, giving them a strangely ghostly appearance against the dark of the sky.

Closer to home the security lights dotted along the paths crossing the hospital grounds poured circles of buttery yellow onto the carpet of white, making it look more like a soft warm blanket than a layer of cold wet snow.

Enough of the warmth of the room behind her had escaped through the curtains to start melting the snow on the window-sill outside, and she grimaced at the thought of days of dirty grey slush while they waited for the thaw.

That had been one item on the news tonight which had received a cheer—when the weather forecaster had promised an early thaw to this unseasonably early snow-fall.

There would undoubtedly be more before the winter was over but as she would be on maternity leave by then with any luck all the severe weather would be over before she was due to return to work.

Although *where* she would be working then was something she didn't dare think about until she and Daniel had found time to finish their interrupted—

Livvy gasped, dragged back to the present moment by the rapid onslaught of the strongest contraction yet. For nearly two minutes she was forced to grip tightly to the edge of the window-sill while she concentrated on relaxing and controlling her breathing.

Resting her forehead against the chill of the window helped a little but it still seemed like for ever before she was able to straighten again and let the curtain drop back into place.

She was almost holding her breath as she walked slowly and carefully across the ward and into Sister's office, still stunned by the enormity of her realisation.

'I'm in labour,' she whispered, as if saying the words aloud would make them more valid. She spread her hands wonderingly over the taut bulge under her smock. 'The baby's really on its way.'

She gave a slightly breathless chuckle as she tried to work out exactly how *long* she'd been in labour.

Now that she knew that it hadn't been Braxton Hicks

contractions she'd been experiencing, she realised that it
was quite possible that things had started slowly some
time this morning and had gradually been speeding up
all day. Those last two had been only twenty minutes
apart, though, the time noted by sheer accident, so that
meant things were beginning to get more serious.

It looked as if she was going to have a Christmas baby
after all.

She glanced around the small, functional room dis-
tractedly, suddenly impatient for things to happen. As a
first baby it could be hours yet, and in the meantime she
knew she wasn't going to be able to rest much and certainly knew she wasn't going to be able to sleep—even
if she hadn't been in labour, the thought that Daniel
would be returning as soon as he'd finished delivering
Alwyn's baby would have kept her awake.

She contemplated perching herself on the edge of the
desk again but her back ached and she knew she needed
the comfort of a real chair for a while. If all the births
she had witnessed were anything to go by, it would be
soon enough that she would be forced to be up and walking about again.

She lowered herself gingerly into the chair, this time
making certain that the cushion was placed just right to
support the hollow of her back before she tilted her head
and tried to relax.

It wasn't long before a sudden thought struck her and
she felt a wide smile creep over her face.

Daniel was actually going to be with her for the birth
of their child.

*That* was something she'd dreamed about during the
last seven months while she'd longed for him to come
to her and demolish the walls that had grown up between

them, but as the time had dragged on without a word from him she'd finally given up hope.

Now he *would* be the first one to hold the baby they'd made together, the one to take it from her body and place it in her arms, the one to marvel with her at the perfection of the tiny fingers and toes and feathery eyelashes.

'Olivia?' said a husky voice near her ear, and she didn't have to open her eyes to know who it was. Only Daniel had ever said her name in exactly that way.

'Daniel,' she murmured, and turned to look at him.

'If you need to go to sleep you'd be better off in bed,' he pointed out gently, smoothing back a straggly tendril of hair to hook it over her ear. He ran the back of his finger down her cheek and Livvy felt her eyes widen as his darkened with awareness.

'I was waiting for you to come back,' she murmured, glad that he hadn't arrived a couple of minutes earlier when she'd been puffing her way through yet another contraction.

Suddenly she remembered where he'd been.

'Alwyn's baby!' she exclaimed, struggling to sit up. 'What happened? Is he all right?'

'He's fine,' Daniel assured her with a grin. 'Perfect, in fact, according to his father.'

'What was the matter with him?' Livvy demanded, remembering the worrying drop in pulse rate with every contraction. 'What did you find when you got in there?'

'He'd managed to wrap the cord round his neck since his last scan—twice!'

'So every time a contraction pushed him a bit further along the birth canal it was getting tighter and tighter and he was getting strangled?' she guessed. 'Poor little boy.'

'It certainly didn't stop him yelling his head off as soon as it was removed,' Daniel pointed out. 'Young Mr Morgan looked quite shell-shocked when he realised there wasn't a volume control on his new toy.'

Livvy chuckled with him, loving the happy expression in his eyes. He was always so genuinely pleased with every baby he delivered. It would be interesting to see how he reacted when this one was born.

She drew in a slow breath and prepared to make the momentous announcement that she was finally in labour. She was looking forward to watching the expression on his face change.

Would he be pleased? Of course he would. He was one of that rare group of men who genuinely loved children rather than tolerated them.

Would he panic because it was *his* child on the way? Maybe. But very few people knew him as well as she did and they probably wouldn't know how to tell. He certainly hadn't seemed in the least bit worried when Davey had been born but, then, he'd only arrived right at the very end of Alice's labour. Perhaps going through it once before would make it easier for him this time.

In the end she had taken so long to start speaking that he beat her to the punch, his voice dragging her away from her convoluted thoughts.

'Livvy, how on earth could you believe that I'd divorced you and married Alice?' he demanded bluntly, and the ocean of quiet hurt in his voice nearly drowned her.

'I sent you the papers,' she reminded him sadly, remembering how angry and unhappy she'd been then. She'd hoped that receiving them would jolt him into seeking her out. 'Or rather the solicitor did.'

'And I tore them up and threw them in the bin—where they belonged.'

'But I didn't know that—you never told me,' Livvy pointed out defensively. 'And when you came here with Alice and she said that she was Mrs Jones and that you'd got married this morning what else was I supposed to think?'

'Well, you should certainly have realised that your solicitor would have been in contact with you to tell you when the case was going to court. How did you think a divorce was conducted?'

'I've got no idea,' she snapped, feeling stupid. 'I've never had one before.'

'Well, you haven't had one this time either,' he said firmly. 'Your name is still Mrs Jones and you're still married to me.'

'But what about Alice?' Livvy persisted. 'She's got that beautiful ring and there *was* a wedding this morning, and what about the baby she's carrying? And there's her little boy, Davey, and your toes and…and…'

'Hey! Hey! Stop and take a breath!' he advised, his tone suddenly teasing as he reached out to grab the straight chair from behind the desk to position it closer to her.

'First things first,' he began with new purpose in his voice. 'Alice *did* get married this morning and she *is* now called Mrs Jones, but you paired her with the wrong man—she married my father.'

'Your father!' Livvy choked in shock. 'But he only lost your mother a few months ago and they'd been married for years.'

'Married and not married,' Daniel pointed out sadly. 'He loved her dearly and cared for her right to the end, but theirs hadn't been a real marriage for a very long time.'

'But Alice?' she questioned. 'How does she fit into all this? And little Davey?'

'Alice was helping Dad to nurse Mum. Inevitably, they ended up spending a lot of time together and they just fell in love.'

'So Davey's *his* son...your half-brother,' she said incredulously. 'And the new baby too?'

'Both of them,' Daniel said, his expression half pride, half bemusement. 'He always wanted a lot of children but I never expected him to start producing the rest of the crop when his oldest was old enough to be producing his own.'

Livvy was silent for a long time while she tried to assimilate everything he'd told her. There was almost too much of it for her to be able to sort everything out in her head.

She had never for one moment considered that Daniel's father could be involved. Although he had warmly welcomed her into the family when she and Daniel had married, and was outwardly a very friendly person, she had recognised a deep well of reserve inside him. He was the last person she would have suspected of conducting an extra-marital affair.

Still, with what Daniel had told her about his parents' marriage, perhaps it wasn't so strange. Even the most reticent of men must have a need for human companionship and physical contact. With the best will in the world, poor Sarah Jones hadn't been able to provide that for years.

Anyway, when she thought about it further, perhaps she should have suspected something like this. After all,

Daniel was so much like his father that she could understand any woman finding him attractive. She'd certainly been bowled over by Daniel—from the first moment she'd met him.

The thing that had really thrown her onto the wrong track had been Daniel's reticence, the way he had refused to explain what was happening. If he had only told her there would have been no need for all this unhappiness.

'What I don't understand is why you didn't explain all of this seven months ago,' she complained bitterly, getting right to the heart of the matter. 'I asked you and asked you to tell me what was going on and all you would do was tell me to trust you. Was it all some elaborate sort of test?'

'God, no!' he exclaimed, and leaned forward to catch her hands in his, holding on tightly in spite of the fact that she tried to snatch them away. 'I wanted to tell you but Alice had sworn me to secrecy.'

'Sworn you to secrecy?' she said in astonishment. 'Why, for heaven's sake?'

'Because she didn't want my father to know that she was pregnant.'

'Why on earth not?' she demanded, exasperated. 'If she loved him enough to go to bed with him what on earth made her think that he wouldn't stand by her when she was pregnant with his child?'

'Firstly, and most importantly, because he was still married to my mother at the time,' Daniel said, staying calm in spite of her anger. 'Alice knew that he would never divorce my mother—she would never have thought of asking him to. But she also knew that it would break his heart to find out that she was pregnant and that he couldn't do anything for her. That's why she wouldn't even let me tell you.'

'But...' Livvy blew out an exasperated breath. She could see Alice's reasoning even though it all seemed very over-dramatic in hindsight. What she wanted to know was how Daniel had become so involved in the situation.

She was just about to ask when he began speaking again, obviously feeling she needed to know some of the background.

'By that time she'd been working for him, and with him, for nearly four years. She would have known better than anyone else how little he was getting out of the marriage and knew how trapped he must be feeling.'

'But he loved your mother,' Livvy objected, remembering the tender, unselfconscious way Daniel's father had fed his helpless wife and read to her from the paper, never once allowing a hint of impatience to colour his voice.

'Yes, he loved her, but it had become more like the protective love of a parent for a child because, really, that's what she'd become. His love for Alice must have taken him completely by surprise after all those years because it was the passionate love of a man for a woman. The age difference between them wouldn't have made the situation any easier for them either.'

'By that time they must both have known that your mother wasn't going to live much longer. Couldn't Alice have told him about the baby on the understanding that she would wait until he was free before they made a commitment? Why did she come to you?'

'She wasn't going to tell him at all,' he said quietly,

releasing her hands and straightening to lean back in the chair.

He rubbed both hands over his face and she could see how deeply weary he was. It must have been such a strain for him, and it obviously wasn't over yet.

She could see from his turbulent expression that he was still fighting demons, and when his gaze dipped to the evidence of the child they had created she realised that he thought she had done a similar thing. Where Alice had concealed her pregnancy from Daniel's father—for whatever reason—she had done the same to Daniel.

In her case, she knew that she hadn't wanted to use her pregnancy to make Daniel feel he had to stay with her, not when she'd believed he'd rather have been with Alice. It had broken her heart to lose him to the other woman that way, but simple pride hadn't let her use the baby to blackmail him into staying.

That reasoning couldn't be the same in Alice's case.

'I still don't understand why she didn't want him to know. You said they were in love and that he's always wanted more children. Surely she would have been giving him everything he'd wanted after half a lifetime in a relationship that was going nowhere.'

'It was because she felt she would be using the baby almost like blackmail,' he said, his words an uncanny echo of her own thoughts a moment ago. 'She knew him well enough to realise that as soon as he found out about the baby he would insist that they got married but she couldn't bear for him to feel that she'd used the baby to trap him.'

He leaned forward again, his expression intent as he tried to make her understand.

'Think about it, Livvy,' he said persuasively. 'She'd seen the way Dad had been trapped for years in a sterile prison, and just when his freedom was in sight—when it looked as if Mum was finally going to be released from her own earthly prison—Alice found out she was pregnant.'

Livvy was silent, his words suddenly making sense.

If she was honest she would probably have made the same decision—in fact, the more she thought about the similarities in their situations the more she realised that she had.

'I understand,' she murmured softly, sadly. 'I can see why she made the decisions she did and I know the thoughts that were going through her head but... I thought you didn't love me any more. I thought you loved her and that the two of you had already started your family.'

'So when you decided to go it was your choice, but it was partly because you thought I'd made *my* choice— that I'd chosen her,' he elaborated, proving that he was just as quick at following verbal clues as she was once they were on the same wavelength.

'I thought that if you really wanted her then I would only be wasting my time if I tried to hold onto you,' she agreed, feeling once again the deep well of unhappiness that had accompanied her on her journey west.

She gave a wry smile, knowing there was no humour in it. 'Mind you, I was also telling myself that if I went away it would make you think seriously about what you really wanted, and if you missed me enough you would leave her in spite of the fact that you'd had a baby to-gether, and come for me.'

'And then I *didn't* come for you,' he said quietly,

reaching for her hand and threading his fingers between hers. 'You couldn't have known that Mum was going to die so soon or that there was going to be a big reorganisation in the department at the hospital to cover Mr den Haag's lecture tour.

'It meant that within days I was absolutely inundated with work at the same time as I was trying to sort out reams of family business.'

'Oh, Daniel,' she murmured, sorry now that she hadn't been there for him when he'd needed her support.

'I was also in contact with Alice and Davey to make sure that she was coping with single motherhood without any friends or relatives to fall back on,' he continued, his remembered frustration clear in his voice.

'I knew she didn't have any family and because she insisted that I keep my promise I couldn't ask anyone else to help out. For weeks before the baby was actually born I was the only one she had to call on for help.'

Hence her insistence on Daniel being there for her son's birth, Livvy thought, remembering how she'd been dreading her own baby arriving without the comfort and support of having Daniel at her side.

She still couldn't understand how the situation had gone on for so long, without her noticing that Daniel was preoccupied with Alice's concerns. But, then, he had also been spending more time visiting his rapidly weakening mother and giving his father some respite from his lonely vigil at her side so perhaps it wasn't so strange.

'All the time I was trying to get her to see that Dad really needed her,' Daniel continued. 'Especially when Mum died. He was absolutely gutted that he'd lost both of them, and that was without knowing that Alice had been carrying his baby. I persuaded her to come to the funeral in the hopes that when she saw him she would change her mind, but she dug in her heels at the last minute.'

'Oh, Daniel, I'm sorry,' she whispered, suddenly overwhelmed by the thought that instead of easing Daniel's problems by going away, she had actually added to them. 'You must have been at your wits' end, trying to sort everything out.'

'And then you had to move to Wales,' he said in disgust. 'What on earth possessed you? Do you have any idea how difficult it is to do any research about medical personnel in an area that far away from St Augustine's? I could hardly jump in the car and spend a quick half-hour on it.

'Do you have any idea how many nurses there are named Jones? Do you have any idea how long it takes to extract their department phone numbers out of personnel departments and then to contact all of them to find out if they're *my* Mrs Jones?'

He glared at her but it wasn't anger she saw in his eyes but the painful echo of...what? Fear?

Livvy was still trying to work it out when he started speaking again, this time his voice strangely unsteady.

'Do you have any idea how frightened I was that I had lost you?' he demanded softly as his hands tightened around hers, his eyes darkened by strong emotions. 'Or how I would have felt if I never saw you again?'

Livvy felt her eyes burn with the press of tears and had to swallow hard as she blinked to force them back.

As she gazed at his dear, handsome face and saw the evidence of the torment his love had put him through, the bands of mistrust around her heart shattered and her own love burst free.

He must have seen the turbulent emotions in her face because suddenly he leapt out of his chair and pulled her to her feet before he gathered her into his arms, protruding stomach and all.

'God, Livvy, I've missed you,' he whispered fervently, as he held her tightly and her head came to rest naturally in its usual place on his shoulder, with his hand stroking her hair. 'I've missed everything about you, you know. Your smile, your laugh, your special perfume even when you aren't wearing any. Everything...'

His head angled towards hers and he met her lips in a kiss that started off sweetly tentative but swiftly escalated to nuclear meltdown.

They were both breathing heavily when he tore his mouth from hers.

'This is impossible,' he groaned as he glanced wildly around. 'Anyone could come in here.'

'And probably will,' Livvy added, only realising the double meaning to their words when she heard his hoarse chuckle.

'I hope that's a promise, Livvy. For God's sake, where's the nearest place we can be alone together? A broom cupboard would do.'

'Daniel, we can't—'

'Pat told me that you've still got a couple of weeks until the baby's due,' he broke in persuasively, a wickedly arousing gleam in his eyes as his fingers began exploratory forays over her shoulders and down towards her tingling breasts. 'That's only two weeks to make up for seven months without the sexiest pregnant woman in the world. It couldn't possibly be enough to make up for all that time without you, but we could do our best to catch up.'

'Yes, but—'

There's less time than you think, she thought as her uterus began to tighten ominously again, but for a few seconds desire overrode the escalating pain.

Yes, she wanted to be alone with him, to make love with him, but she didn't think it was advisable or even possible while she was in labour.

'And you know as well as I do that making love in the last few weeks of pregnancy helps to ripen the cervix.' He continued to argue eloquently as he covered her face with kisses and slid his hands down the length of her back to palm the curves of her hips. 'It could actually be good for you.'

'Oh, Daniel,' Livvy whimpered helplessly as her body clenched tightly with a combination of desire and her strongest contraction yet, then felt a strange release of tension.

She buried her face against his shoulder and moaned, half in laughter and half in frustration.

'Oh, Daniel, I'd love to go with you to the nearest private place and make mad, passionate love—I'd even be willing to make do with a broom cupboard—but I think my waters just broke.'

# CHAPTER TEN

LIVVY cradled the precious bundle in her arms and glanced over her shoulder at Daniel.

'Does he know we're coming?' she demanded, suspicious of the barely contained glee in his expression as he pushed the wheelchair towards the entrance of the orthopaedic ward.

It seemed awfully early to be going visiting. Daniel probably wouldn't have been allowed to do it if he wasn't a doctor and she wasn't a member of staff.

Breakfast was hardly over but from the moment the main lights had come on in the ward it had been filled with a real air of excitement.

It wasn't just because it was Christmas Day but also because once the curtains had been drawn back everyone had seen that the snow had virtually disappeared overnight and several patients had been told they would be allowed to go home today.

As for the rest, they now knew that the roads would be clear enough for their families to be able to visit them so everyone was feeling much happier.

'He'll know we're coming soon enough,' Daniel said with a grin as he expertly reversed through the swing doors and swung her gently back to face the room.

The first person she saw on the other side of the room was Alice, who was sitting on the chair tucked closely beside the bed, her hand tightly held by the man she was visiting.

Perched on the edge of the bed between them was a young child who bore a startling similarity both to the man confined to the bed and the one behind her, pushing the wheelchair.

'Hello, Dad,' Daniel said softly when the older man didn't seem to have noticed their arrival at the end of his bed. He apparently only had eyes for the radiant woman by his side and the bonny young lad propped between them.

'Daniel?'

The older man's expression was startled and only grew more so when he recognised the person sitting in the wheelchair at the foot of his bed.

'Livvy? Is that you?' he demanded, a beam of pleasure filling his face. 'What on earth are you...?'

He paused, doing a visible double-take when he saw what she was holding in her arms.

'My God! Is that *yours*? Daniel told me you were pregnant but when did that happen?'

Daniel laughed at his less than elegant speech.

'It certainly is ours, *Grandad*. Born just a minute before midnight.'

David Jones still didn't seem to be able to take it in, his eyes going from one face to the other almost as if he expected them to disappear as quickly as they'd come.

'Until Daniel told me yesterday, I didn't even know Livvy was pregnant,' he complained to Alice, sounding almost bewildered. 'I know I was pretty much out of it on anaesthetic but I'm sure I hadn't heard that the two of them were together again—not that I knew why they parted in the first place.'

'That makes three of us,' Daniel muttered in an aside

to Livvy, who couldn't help the wide smile that spread over her face.

'We're definitely together again,' she said, reaching up one hand to weave her fingers between Daniel's. 'We just thought you'd like to meet the latest addition to the Jones family.'

'*He* just wanted a chance to crow,' Daniel's father accused wryly. 'Did you hear the emphasis he put on the word *Grandad*? And here I was congratulating myself that people would think I was just a youngster to have such a pretty wife and several small children.'

'Several?' Alice echoed, trying to sound horrified. 'The last I heard it was just one-and-a-bit children, and I've got the ultrasound picture to prove it.'

'So far,' David agreed with a roguish look which was uncannily like his oldest son's.

'You do realise that you're going to be crossing the generations over with this next one,' Daniel pointed out. 'By the time your second one is born it will already be an uncle or aunt to ours.'

The situation sounded so strange that they all laughed.

'So, what did you have?' David prompted. 'I've an idea that Alice already knows because she's been in a funny mood ever since she brought Davey in to visit.'

Alice shared a secretive smile with Livvy. Everyone on the ward had found out the sex of the baby within seconds of the birth but she'd obviously decided to let Daniel break the news to his father.

'It's a girl,' Daniel announced with a besotted grin as he turned to lift his daughter carefully out of Livvy's arms.

He turned to carry her round the end of the bed for

inspection with all the confidence of a man who knew that he would meet with approval.

Livvy hid her amusement when she saw the extra care he took as he held their child. No one would have guessed, from the exaggerated precautions he was taking to support her head as he handed her over to his father, that he was well accustomed to dealing with tiny babies...but, then, this really was the first one that was *his*.

'Have you decided yet what you're going to call her?' David asked, glancing up at them briefly as he stroked one petal-soft cheek with a gentle finger.

Daniel had returned to Livvy's side and threw a quick look at her, as though he was waiting for her to answer, but she gestured for him to do it, tightening her hand around his in loving support.

'We thought we'd like to call her Sarah—after Mum—if you've no objection?' he suggested softly.

Silence surrounded their little gathering for several long seconds while David looked searchingly from one to another, ending up with Alice.

As Livvy watched, she saw the silent communication that passed between the two of them and it was Alice who answered.

'That's a lovely idea,' she whispered as she reached out to stroke a gentle hand over the silky blonde wisps covering the new baby's head. 'A beautiful name for a beautiful baby, and one that will help to keep all the good memories alive.'

Young Davey chose that moment to try to wriggle off the bed and Alice had to grab him before he nose-dived towards the floor.

In the ensuing exclamations and laughter conversation became more general, encompassing the possibilities of transferring David closer to home—preferably to St Augustine's, where Daniel would be able to help Alice with visiting—and questions about Livvy's plans for returning to work.

'We haven't got that far yet,' Livvy confessed honestly. 'It's a bit of a long story, but the only thing we're certain about at the moment is that I'll be going back home with Daniel as soon as I'm released from here.'

'Well, with Daniel as your doctor, you can virtually sign your own release,' David pointed out with a chuckle as he relinquished his hold on his first grandchild with every evidence of regret. 'I'm not going to be quite so lucky. Our honeymoon is going to have to be put off for the foreseeable future—and just when we'd persuaded my cousin to take Davey on for the duration!'

'Theoretically, Livvy could be released today as her labour was so perfectly straightforward, but it's not quite as simple as that,' Daniel said, and explained briefly about the staff shortages on the obstetrics and gynaecology wards.

'One down with flu, one with his arm in plaster and another on a skiing holiday?' David said. 'I bet the last one is kicking himself. He could have had free skiing in his own back garden and saved himself a lot of money.'

'Well, he's not due back for another four days, and as I'd already arranged to take some time off from St Augustine's I thought I might as well pitch in at Bryn Madoc,' Daniel explained. 'At least it means I'll be able to see something of Livvy at the same time.'

'It's not quite the same as being at home, though,' Alice pointed out. 'There'll be no privacy at all.'

'There's always the broom cupboard,' Daniel said with an attempt at a straight face, but Livvy knew the colour that surged up into her face had given her thoughts away when David's eyebrows shot up towards his hairline.

'We'd better take Sarah back to the nursery or we'll be in trouble,' she pointed out hurriedly, before Daniel's father could comment on the cause of her embarrassment. His thought processes certainly weren't being slowed down by anaesthetic today and he was intelligent enough to make a fairly accurate guess.

'Lord, yes,' Daniel agreed when he glanced at his watch. 'I've got to track down that wretched Santa suit before I can give out the presents on the ward.'

Livvy couldn't help chuckling at the idea of Daniel disguised under pounds of padding and a full white beard, but she knew that the mums who were expecting their young families to visit were delighted by the idea.

When they were travelling back up in the lift she tried to scold Daniel for mentioning the broom cupboard but he silenced her with a sizzling kiss.

'We never even got as far as the broom cupboard so don't take away my fantasies,' he murmured. 'Now that you're off limits for a while they're all that I've got.'

Livvy's brains were so scrambled by his kiss that she couldn't reply, but as the doors opened just then to reveal a group of people waiting to enter the lift, it hardly mattered.

There would be time enough to remind him of all the things they *would* be able to do when they didn't have an audience.

Their return to the ward coincided with the arrival of a whole group of relatives, including Megan Williams's little boys.

For a while the three of them were overawed enough by their surroundings to stay quietly by her bed, but it wasn't long before they became brave enough to start exploring the ward and introducing themselves to all the other patients.

Livvy had settled herself back into bed and was eagerly waiting for Daniel to return from his 'duties' as Father Christmas on the ward upstairs when the two bravest of the sturdy imps reached her.

'You're not fat,' announced the older of the two. 'Didn't you get a baby?'

'Yes. I had a little girl,' Livvy said, side-stepping the issue of size. She'd been amazed and delighted when she'd sneaked onto the scales this morning to find that she was going to have to lose less than four pounds to get back to her pre-pregnancy weight. She'd been convinced when it felt as if she left dents in the floor just by walking, that it was going to be a great deal more than that.

Unfortunately, most women weren't nearly so lucky...

'Oh!' said young Master Williams in tones of commiseration. 'We had a girl too.'

Livvy didn't know how she stopped herself laughing. The poor lad had made it sound as if he equated the arrival of a baby sister in the family with the offer of a plate of snails for breakfast.

Daniel's reaction had been very different when their daughter had been born late last night.

Her announcement that her waters had broken had stunned him, but not nearly as much as the realisation, when he'd looked down at his shoes, that he was just as drenched as she was.

'Livvy!' he'd exclaimed, his ardour definitely damp-
ened. 'I've heard of pouring cold water on an idea but
this is going too far. If you didn't want to come in the
broom cupboard with me all you had to do was say so!'

Livvy had already been chuckling so hard at his expression that the contraction had completely robbed her
of breath.

By the time she'd been able to speak again he'd found
a wheelchair and grabbed Cherry to take her off to get
rid of her wet clothing and put her in a gown.

The young nurse had been strangely quiet while she'd
helped Livvy make herself comfortable, but she'd waited
until the relative quiet between contractions before she'd
dropped her bombshell.

'I'm having second thoughts about my speciality,' she
announced, hardly able to meet Livvy's eyes.

'Oh, Cherry, why?' Livvy demanded. 'You've got
good instincts, you're calm and steady with the patients
and you've coped marvellously with everything that's
happened over the last couple of days, even though it's
been chaotic.'

'That's partly why,' she said quietly. 'The last couple
of days have been fantastic, with everything happening
at once, and I've thoroughly enjoyed myself. But I think
it mightn't be so interesting when everything gets back
to normal and it's all peaceful and well organised.'

'Normal? Peaceful and well organised?' Livvy chuckled breathlessly, trying to relax and control her breathing
as the next contraction roared towards her like an express train. 'You must be joking! This *is* normal for a
maternity ward!'

'What? But...' Cherry was clearly at a loss.

'Think about it,' Livvy gasped. 'No one has yet found

a way of persuading babies to arrive to order... There are no neat lists of operations... You never know when the next mum is going to arrive in labour, day or night... Or if there are going to be half a dozen at once... Or how long each one is going to take... Disorganised chaos every time...' she finished with an agonised groan.

'And she loves every minute of it,' Daniel announced as he joined them, this time dressed in a baggy pair of blue theatre scrubs.

'Delivering other people's babies,' Livvy pointed out through gritted teeth, 'is much easier than do-it-yourself...'

Cherry laughed, her eyes once more bright and enthusiastic as she gathered up Livvy's clothes into a large damp bundle.

'I can see I shall have to do a rethink—about my career *and* my thoughts about having babies of my own,' she announced as she disappeared out of the swing doors.

'How is it going?' Daniel asked as he blotted the sweat off Livvy's face and stroked the clinging hairs away to make her comfortable.

'I'd rather be in the broom cupboard,' she muttered crossly as he held some water for her to take a mouthful. She'd only had a sip when she was seized with the uncontrollable urge to push. 'On second thoughts, what you were suggesting we did in the broom cupboard was what got me into this situation,' she said, her voice rising rapidly like a kettle coming to the boil. 'If you so much as mention broom cupboards again I'll—'

'Livvy?' Daniel said sharply, cutting her off in full flow.

'Yes?' she snapped, glaring up at him, uncomfortably aware that she was behaving like a shrew.

'Shut up and push.'

Livvy could laugh about it now, especially as Daniel had threatened to tease her about broom cupboards for the rest of her life.

The rest of her life... She gave a happy sigh. It seemed impossible that so much had changed in the space of a day.

Yesterday she had been alone and lonely with only the prospect of the birth of her baby in the New Year to look forward to. Today she was the mother of a perfect baby girl and had the absolute certainty that she was never going to be alone or lonely again.

Guiltily she realised that her lack of interest in their conversation had prompted Megan Williams's sons to move on to more interesting people.

She was just looking around the ward to see where they were now when a commotion just outside the doors to the ward drew everyone's attention.

'Ho! Ho! Ho!' said a voice as the doors slowly opened.

'It's Father Christmas!' exclaimed one of the junior Williamses in a piercing whisper when he caught sight of the familiar red-clad figure in the doorway.

Livvy threw him a quick glance and saw that the little child's eyes were almost standing out on stalks with excitement, and his brothers were just as amazed.

She looked back in time to see Daniel appear, his shape so completely disguised that if she hadn't known it was him under the suit there would have been no way of telling.

This was a Father Christmas with a difference, though. Instead of the traditional sack of brightly wrapped parcels slung over his back, this Father Christmas was carrying a double armful of babies.

'Wow!' breathed another junior Williams, every bit as awed as his brothers. 'He's giving out *babies* for presents!'

There was a ripple of laughter around the ward, including one from Father Christmas himself as he made his way to Jo Moffat's bed.

'I've got two presents for you,' Father Christmas announced. 'Baby David is the first one.'

He leaned forward so that Jo could lift her little boy out of his hold and cradle him in her arms. She obviously hadn't understood what he'd meant about two presents because she was looking up at him with a puzzled frown.

'You'll have to look towards the door for your second surprise,' he prompted.

Jo's head swung towards the doors, now framing a rather rumpled-looking man, and she burst into tears.

'In case any of you are wondering,' Father Christmas announced to the rest of the room, 'her husband has managed to get some leave to be with her for Christmas.'

He moved out of the way to allow husband and wife to embrace around their new son and moved on to Nerys Owens's bed.

Nerys and John didn't need any special gifts—their baby was obviously all they wanted as the proud new father perched on the edge of the bed to share a cuddle.

Alwyn Morgan was almost as overwhelmed as the Williams children, still hardly daring to believe that her baby really was alive and safely in her arms.

'Now, then, who have we here?' Father Christmas asked as he arrived at Megan Williams's bed.

In the time that it had taken him to work his way round there, the two boys had hurried over to station themselves beside their father and their younger sibling.

'This is the Williams family, Father Christmas,' Megan announced seriously.

'Well, then, this must be your special delivery,' he announced as he handed over Megan's precious daughter, all snugly wrapped in a pale pink blanket.

'We got a *girl*,' the oldest boy whispered loudly to his father. 'I wanted Father Christmas to change it for a boy but he only had girls left.'

Livvy could see that Daniel was fighting laughter but the rest of the ward was free to chuckle aloud.

She straightened as he settled his final delivery securely in the crook of his scarlet-coated arm and set off towards her, only to veer towards the door.

'Hey! Was that a spare one?' called a sharp-eyed child. Livvy didn't see which one it was—she was too busy watching to see what Daniel was doing with their daughter.

He paused in the doorway to reach up over his head and grab the mistletoe, then turned to make his way towards her.

'What's he going to do with that?' demanded the same little voice.

Livvy didn't bother to listen to the explanation. She *knew* what Daniel was intending to do with the mistletoe—giving himself an excuse to kiss her in front of all these people.

'Ho! Ho! Ho!' he said softly as he reached her side. 'And have you been a good girl?'

'Of course I have, Father Christmas,' she answered demurely.

She nearly burst out laughing when he leaned closer to mutter, 'Unfortunately... But I hope you'll do better next year!'

He carefully transferred Sarah to her arms and ostentatiously held the sprig of green leaves and waxy white berries over the baby's head.

'Happy Christmas,' he said as he placed a whiskery kiss on the soft curve of the baby's cheek.

He looked up to meet Livvy's eyes and his softly loving expression darkened and suddenly became heated.

'And a very happy Christmas to you, Livvy,' he murmured as he leaned towards her. 'I love you.'

At the very last moment, when his raised arm clad in voluminous red hid their faces from the rest of the room, he tugged his beard out of the way and their lips met.

Without a word their mouths spoke of happiness and for ever, gradually extending the vocabulary to include desire and searing passion, but once again it was the piercing whisper of a little boy that brought everything back to earth.

'What's Father Christmas doing?' he demanded, and Daniel groaned softly into Livvy's mouth as he was forced to bring their kiss to an end.

'He's giving her a kiss to wish her a happy Christmas,' Megan Williams explained simply, then, obviously knowing her son well, she added, 'It's all right. She's Mrs Christmas.'

Livvy hid her burning face against Daniel's shoulder, certain that her cheeks must be the same colour as his coat.

'Hey, how did I do on my first foray as Father

Christmas?' Daniel asked, his beard once more in position. 'I thought it would be a good idea to get some practice before Sarah's old enough to be critical.'

'You were the perfect instant Father Christmas,' Livvy teased.

Daniel's gaze fell on their daughter, sleeping peacefully between them.

'Instant father, too,' he murmured. 'I didn't have time to get stage fright or have second thoughts.'

'A bit like the way you do most of the really important things in your life,' she pointed out. 'You proposed just weeks after we met, but I bet you never thought you'd manage one day of father-to-be before the big event.'

'There are certainly *some* advantages,' he agreed, 'but next time can we do things the traditional way, with a nine-month lead-in?'

'Next time?' she demanded. 'You can mention next time when it's less than twelve hours since I went through agony to bring this one into the world.'

'Ah, but remember how much fun we had, putting her there in the first place,' he murmured, the wicked twinkle in his eye nothing to do with cuddly old Father Christmas.

'Go and take your clothes off and we'll talk about it when you come back,' she prompted, needing to see her beloved Daniel beside her when he was saying such outrageous things.

'If I took my clothes off now *everyone* would have something to talk about,' he said gruffly, but he slid off the edge of the bed and surreptitiously rearranged his robes. 'I'll be back in a few minutes with the rest of the children's presents—the dads left them in a pile in the corner by the lift—but I've been asked to do the ceremonial turkey-carving a bit later on so we're not going to have much time together.'

Livvy knew hospital life too well to complain, but she would have liked their first day together with their new baby to have had a little more opportunity for privacy.

It wasn't until just before he was due to carve the turkey for lunch that Daniel, in his own persona, handed her a plain white envelope with a whispered, 'Happy Christmas.'

Intrigued, Livvy untucked the flap and drew out a single sheet of hospital stationery and a key.

'Oh, Daniel,' she squeaked when she'd read the contents. 'When?'

'The administrator said he can have the flat ready for me to move into by this evening,' he explained. 'I went to ask him if there was anywhere I could lay my weary head, in between delivering all these babies, and I just happened to mention that my wife was on the staff here and that she'd just had her first baby unexpectedly early and—'

And they've found you somewhere to stay while you're helping out,' Livvy finished.

'Actually, it's somewhere for *us* to stay,' he said with a flash of that familiar grin. 'I just couldn't wait any longer to have my instant family all to myself.'

'You may have been an instant Father Christmas and an instant father,' Livvy began softly, sliding her fingers between his so that the key was enclosed between their palms, 'but from now on we're going to work hard to make certain that it's going to be for-ever-after love and happiness.'

'That's a promise,' Daniel said, and leaned forward to

brush a chaste kiss over her lips. He had to draw back in a hurry when a horrified whisper pierced the general hubbub of the ward.

'Mummy! He's kissing Mrs Christmas!'

# MILLS & BOON®

# *M*akes
## any time
## special

## Enjoy a romantic novel from
## Mills & Boon®

*Presents*™ *Enchanted*™ *Temptation*®

*Historical Romance*™ *Medical Romance*™

# MILLS & BOON®

## Next Month's Romance Titles

♡

Each month you can choose from a wide variety of romance novels from Mills & Boon®. Below are the new titles to look out for next month from the Presents™ and Enchanted™ series.

### *Presents*™

| | |
|---|---|
| TO WOO A WIFE | Carole Mortimer |
| CONTRACT BABY | Lynne Graham |
| IN BED WITH THE BOSS | Susan Napier |
| SURRENDER TO SEDUCTION | Robyn Donald |
| OUTBACK MISTRESS | Lindsay Armstrong |
| THE SECRET DAUGHTER | Catherine Spencer |
| THE MARRIAGE ASSIGNMENT | Alison Kelly |
| WIFE BY AGREEMENT | Kim Lawrence |

### *Enchanted*™

| | |
|---|---|
| BE MY GIRL! | Lucy Gordon |
| LONESOME COWBOY | Debbie Macomber |
| A SUITABLE GROOM | Liz Fielding |
| NEW YEAR...NEW FAMILY | Grace Green |
| OUTBACK HUSBAND | Jessica Hart |
| MAKE-BELIEVE MOTHER | Pamela Bauer & Judy Kaye |
| OH, BABY! | Lauryn Chandler |
| FOLLOW THAT GROOM! | Christie Ridgway |

On sale from 8th January 1999

H1 9812

*Available at most branches of WH Smith, Tesco, Asda, Martins, Borders and all good paperback bookshops*

**MILLS & BOON®**

*Makes any time special™*

*By Request*

### Bestselling themed romances brought back to you by popular demand

Each month By Request brings you three full-length novels in one beautiful volume featuring the best of the best.

So if you missed a favourite Romance the first time around, here is your chance to relive the magic from some of our most popular authors.

**Look out for**
***Blind Passions* in January 1999**
**featuring Miranda Lee,**
**Rebecca Winters and Emma Goldrick**

*Available at most branches of WH Smith, Tesco, Asda, Martins, Borders, Easons, Volume One/James Thin and most good paperback bookshops*

*We are giving away a year's supply of Mills & Boon® books to the five lucky winners of our latest competition. Simply match the six film stars to the films in which they appeared, complete the coupon overleaf and send this entire page to us by 30th June 1999. The first five correct entries will each win a year's subscription to the Mills & Boon series of their choice. What could be easier?*

| | | |
|---|---|---|
| **CABARET** ___ | **GONE WITH THE WIND** ___ | |
| **ROCKY** ___ | **SMOKEY & THE BANDIT** ___ | |
| **PRETTY WOMAN** ___ | **GHOST** ___ | |

C8L

**Please turn over for details of how to enter →**

# HOW TO ENTER

There are six famous faces and a list of six films overleaf. Each of the famous faces starred in one of the films listed and all you have to do is match them up!

As you match each one, write the number of the actor or actress who starred in each film in the space provided. When you have matched them all, fill in the coupon below, pop this page in an envelope and post it today. Don't forget you could win a year's supply of Mills & Boon® books—you don't even need to pay for a stamp!

Mills & Boon Hollywood Heroes Competition
FREEPOST CN81, Croydon, Surrey, CR9 3WZ
EIRE readers: (please affix stamp) PO Box 4546, Dublin 24.

Please tick the series you would like to receive if you
are one of the lucky winners

Presents™ ❏  Enchanted™ ❏  Historical Romance™ ❏

Medical Romance™ ❏  Temptation® ❏

Are you a Reader Service™ subscriber?     Yes ❏     No ❏

Ms/Mrs/Miss/Mr ................Initials ...........................
                                                (BLOCK CAPITALS PLEASE)
Surname........................................................................

Address ......................................................................

................................................................................

................................................Postcode...........................

(I am over 18 years of age)                                        C8L

Closing date for entries is 30th June 1999. One entry per household. Free subscriptions are for four books per month. Competition open to residents of the UK and Ireland only. As a result of this application, you may receive further offers from Harlequin Mills & Boon and other carefully selected companies. If you would prefer not to share in this opportunity please write to The Data Manager at the address shown above.

Mills & Boon is a registered trademark of
Harlequin Mills & Boon Ltd.